W9-CFB-017

THE ZUCCHINI CONSPIRACY

★ THE ★
ZUCCHINI
CONSPIRACY

A NOVEL OF ALTERNATIVE FACTS

TIMOTHY BALDING

UPPER WEST SIDE PHILOSOPHERS, INC.

NEW YORK

Upper West Side Philosophers, Inc. provides a publication venue for original philosophical thinking steeped in lived life, in line with our motto: philosophical living & lived philosophy.

Published by Upper West Side Philosophers, Inc. / P. O. Box 250645, New York, NY 10025, USA
www.westside-philosophers.com / www.yogaforthemind.us

First US Edition.
The Zucchini Conspiracy is published simultaneously in the UK and USA.

The colophon is a registered trademark
of Upper West Side Philosophers, Inc.

Yoga for the Mind®

Library of Congress Cataloging-in-Publication Data

Names: Balding, Timothy, 1954- author.
Title: The zucchini conspiracy : a novel of alternative facts / Timothy Balding.
Description: New York : Upper West Side Philosophers, Inc., 2019.
Identifiers: LCCN 2019026584 (print) | LCCN 2019026585 (ebook) | ISBN 9781935830672 (trade paperback) | ISBN 9781935830689 (epub)
Subjects: LCSH: Political fiction. | GSAFD: Fantasy fiction
Classification: LCC PR9105.9.B35 Z83 2019 (print) | LCC PR9105.9.B35 (ebook) | DDC 823/.92--dc23
LC record available at https://lccn.loc.gov/2019026584
LC ebook record available at https://lccn.loc.gov/2019026585

Design: UWSP, Inc.
Cover Art & Design: Rui Ricardo / Folio Art

A UWSP Original Softcover

THE ZUCCHINI CONSPIRACY

CAST OF CHARACTERS

Ronald Rump, President of the United States, a legend in his own mind

Hakim Akim, avaricious Dictator of Bangistan, disciple of King **Mansu Musa** of Mali

Holden, US Secretary of State, a scheming warmonger

Yogi Akim, aka **Henry Tate**, evil, duplicitous brother of Bangistan's Great Leader

Emmanuel, **Angela**, **Giuseppe**, **Justin**, **Shinzo** and **Theresa**, world leaders with a brave and dubious plan

Dan O'Reilly, loyal (up to a point) Director of the CIA

Zebriski, US Secretary of Defense, a pacifist

Winkelmeier, reluctant US Ambassador to Petrobangorski

Vladimir Putin & **Xi Jinping**, respective Presidents of Russia and China, standing jokes

Olga, professional flagellator at the Edelweiss Boom Boom Club

Dmitry Ilyich Bogdanov, devout hermit Commander of the Bangistani nuclear weapons base

Sir Edmund Pickering, lascivious British Ambassador to France

Stephen Blakely, idealistic First Secretary to the British Embassy in Paris, and his wife **Ruth**

Scott Schurz, his amusing US Embassy counterpart

George Ormrod, UK Foreign Secretary, rising star of British politics

Sally, Ormrod's sardonic PA

Stavros Kamaras, disputatious Greek Culture Minister

Charles Roche la Molière, French Culture Minister, mocker of the English

Marie-Pierre Etxeberria, prize-winning Gascon zucchini cultivator

Gaston Etxeberria, long-suffering husband and interpreter for Marie-Pierre

Monsieur Lizarazu, six times Mayor of Luchère-Les-Bains, a great wit

Irène, a Basque innkeeper, the Mayor's accomplice in humor

Hawkins, professional photographer, suspected British spy

Frank Fitman, physician to the US President

Adela Laperye, French secret agent, polyglot

Pierre Morand, French secret agent, truck driver

Several **Bangistani interpreters** of questionable competence

General Gianfranco Geppetto, philandering Italian spy-master, and his foreign intelligence colleagues, **Gilles Haubois, Marshal Tuoma Nakajima, Sir Harry Peterson, Robert Pensec, Vincent Collins** and **Major General Hans Hopfinger**

Malabo, a very distinguished gorilla

AUTHOR'S INTRODUCTION

"For evil to flourish, it only requires good men to do nothing."

This common political adage has been attributed to numerous, worthy persons, none of whom actually said it. But no matter. Whatever their origin, lost in history, the words are wise and indubitably true.

The story that you are about to read recounts the actions of a small group of brave, perhaps heroic, individuals who decided that they *must* act in the face of iniquity and turpitude, *must* fight to counter an evil that could quite possibly lead to war and to mass destruction.

It was Dicky Dickson*, a former janitor at the US Department of State, who encouraged me to write this book. A distant Scottish relative, it was he who stumbled upon a file that, though marked 'Classified – Top Secret', had somehow ended up in an office garbage can. It had just one word written across its cover: 'Zucchini'.

Dicky quite rightly thought that it was his solemn duty, and, perhaps, in his pecuniary interest, to share with the world the extraordinary information that the file contained, and, since he knew I was a writer, he entrusted me with this task.

The events in this novel took place in the spring and early summer of 2019. The Zucchini dossier itself told only the bare bones of this extravagant story. I have thus invented and fictionalized the rest of it, giving full rein to my overwrought imagination.

* *Name changed*

It goes without saying that I have been obliged to modify names, places and dates to disguise the identity of many of the real protagonists. My most discerning readers will see, nevertheless, that other characters loosely resemble prominent, known personalities and that I have done little to conceal this. In these cases, I have concluded that the men and women in question can quite well take care of themselves and, above all, are unlikely to sue my most excellent publishers.

Timothy Balding

CHAPTER 1

PEACE IN OUR TIME

Ronald Rump pulled up both his trouser legs to the knee and scratched furiously. He then thrust one of his hands under his shirt and clawed wildly at his chest.

"What's the point of being the most powerful man in the most powerful country in the world if you are being eaten alive by rash?" yelled the President at the bevy of officials shuffling into his office. "Why the fuck can't some one fix this?!"

Rump had already fired three of his physicians whose pills and creams had brought no relief at all to his skin ailments. His new doctor, Frank Fitman, had told him that the problem was 'psychosomatic', whatever the hell that meant. All he could advise was that the President should forget Bangistan for a few days and go and play golf. I'm not going to keep this one any longer than the others, the President had already promised himself.

"What's the latest, Ambassador?" asked Rump, gripping his desk with both hands to place them temporarily out of reach of his itches. "Are we on, finally?"

"There's a major new obstacle, I'm afraid, Mr. President," replied the Ambassador, taking a seat in front of Rump. "Akim now says that he won't meet at all if you insist on bringing – please excuse the direct quote, Mr. Secretary – that 'evil piece of shit Holden' with you."

The President laughed. "Evil piece of shit? He really said *that*?"

"Yes, Sir. Although the expression was a little more elaborate in Bangistani. It involved goats and … your mother."

"*My* mother?! That son of a bitch. Why not Holden's mother?"

"I don't know, Sir."

"All I can say," said Rump, leaning back in his chair, "is that Akim is a pretty good judge of character!"

The only person in the room who did not join the President in the rush of laughter was Secretary of State Holden. He would have liked to, just to please Rump, but his range of sentiments unfortunately did not extend to mirth.

Encouraged by this better-than-expected reception for his message from the Bangistani capital, the Ambassador felt he could permit himself to add: "To quote Akim in full, Sir, he did also say that he regretted that Secretary Holden was not *their* 'evil piece of shit' but ours, and that he could be enjoying a much more successful career with them."

"That's a compliment, Holden," said the President. Keen to see the Secretary squirm a bit more, and unwilling to give up yet his successful joke, he continued: "Maybe we could make an exchange? Who's Holden's counterpart, Ambassador?"

"Yogi Akim, Sir. A very bad man."

"*Yogi*? What kind of name is *that*? Doesn't sound very Bangistani to me, not that I know much about their dumb language. Nothing, to be precise."

"You're quite right, Mr. President. It seems that his father – *their* father, in fact; he's Hakim's younger brother – was a baseball fan. He adored the New York Yankees and especially Yogi Berra."

"What a strange world," mused the President. "Someone make a note to include that in my brief for the trip. Let's present him with a Yankees cap – it's that kind of thing that clinches deals, you know."

Ambassador Winkelmeier, Holden, the Secretary of Defense, the CIA Director and the other officials who huddled around Rump's desk, nodded solemnly in agreement with this Presidential wisdom.

"So, when are we going? When can we schedule the meeting, assuming I agree to leave Holden behind?" asked the President.

The men looked uneasily at each other and cleared their throats noisily.

"Ambassador?" suggested Holden.

Winkelmeier took a deep breath. "There are several other conditions to consider before we can decide that, Sir. He's making a lot, actually."

"Conditions? We're giving that little runt a chance to meet the President of the United States of America and he's setting *conditions*? Doesn't he know that I could blow his shithole country off the face of the earth with a wave of my hand?"

"Yes, Sir," said the Ambassador. "I did insist on that, reminded him of your threats in this respect, but he didn't seem impressed."

"*Impressed*? I'm sure you're far too polite with him, too diplomatic, Winkelmeier. Wait until I get hold of him. He'll soon learn who's calling the tune. In any case, tell us about these so-called *conditions*," said Rump, spitting out the word with deep loathing.

Where might I start? wondered the Ambassador, a rather gentle soul who greatly feared the President's displeasure. He had not wanted to go to Bangistan in the first place, so far was it from his beloved Georgetown and its cobblestone sidewalks, but one did not, after all, join the foreign service to stay at home, and he had acquiesced when the post had been proposed to him. It had all been the fault of Mrs. Winkelmeier, in fact, who in the hope of pushing her husband's stagnating career along a little, had blabbed gushingly about his knowledge of former Soviet satellite nations to a complete stranger at a post-inauguration cocktail party. How this had found its way to the ear of the President, or whoever decided these matters, he would never know.

"Come on, come on," urged Rump, as the Ambassador hesitated.

"Well, Mr. President, you're not going to believe this …"

"Try me," the impatient Rump interrupted.

"Akim insists that you should be accompanied at the meeting by Robert De Niro."

"De Niro, the actor? He hates my guts, he'd never agree."

A little astonished that the President had deigned to take this condition seriously, Winkelmeier quickly added: "He did say that if De Niro wasn't available, he'd settle for George Clooney."

"And the rest of my Hollywood fan club, I suppose? Why the hell couldn't he choose an actor who likes me?"

Ambassador Winkelmeier well remembered that he had personally tried to identify one such man or woman to propose to Akim. He had failed, but thought it best to keep this information to himself.

"What else?" asked the President. "I suppose he wants us to give up our nuclear weapons too?!" he chortled with glee.

"Yes, Sir, he does, actually," said Defense Secretary Zebriski. "Those in Europe, at least."

"We have nuclear weapons in Europe?!" exclaimed Rump. "Are you sure, Zebriski?"

"Yes, Sir, quite sure."

"Who's paying for them?"

"We are, Sir. They're ours, after all."

Anticipating the President's next reflection, he added swiftly: "But if we actually use them, in the defense of our allies, of course, they'll pay us back."

"I damn well hope so," said Rump curtly. "Those babies cost a lot of money. How much a head, Zebriski?"

"A head, Sir?"

"A warhead," quipped Rump, pleased with his little wordplay.

"More than fifty million dollars each," said the Secretary. "I haven't got an exact figure, though I could get you one, of course."

"Have we got our latest in there? The BW ... what was it?"

"We can't talk about that, Mr. President, I'm afraid," CIA Director O'Reilly intervened sharply. "It's a secret, classified."

"We keep secrets from ourselves?"

"Let's say the fewer who are aware of the details, the better," said O'Reilly, casting an unpleasant look over his colleagues.

Rump suddenly spun round on his chair and peered out of the Oval Office window at the lawns. He mumbled something that the others strained to hear. They stared at each other quizzically as O'Reilly whispered to Holden: "I think he said 'Nice green'." He was happy that further discussion of warhead specifics had been averted by the President's horticultural observations, and seized the moment to get back to the subject of negotiations.

"Sir, Mr. President, perhaps the best way forward would be to ask Ambassador Winkelmeier to give you a full rundown on his discussions with Akim."

The President turned back to the room, yawned, nodded his assent, and instructed: "Just make it brief."

"That's not difficult, Mr. President," began Winkelmeier. "We did not, of course, discuss anything detailed, or substantive. Since you've both agreed to the principle of a meeting, my only concern was to establish Akim's minimal … his minimal … *caveats* for going forward with it."

The Ambassador was pleased with himself for having averted the irritating word 'conditions' and for coming up with an alternative that he was pretty sure lay outside the President's vocabulary and, thus, offense.

"Anyhow, what does he want me to do, apart from sending Holden to the movies and making De Niro Secretary of State?" asked Rump. "Not to mention the little matter of taking our nukes out of Europe."

"Well, Sir, it turns out that Akim is afraid to travel at present. It's not fear of flying, or anything like that, but as far as I understand, reading between the lines, he's terrified of a coup or something happening in his absence. I can't understand why, since all his opponents have been executed or are chained up in prison. Paranoia, I suppose, a common affliction among dictators. But since he really can't leave the country …"

"You're not suggesting, of course, that the President go to Bangistan?" Holden broke in rudely. "Absolutely out of the question," O'Reilly added with a dismissive laugh. "A definite no-no."

"Hold your horses," said the President. "I decide these things, not you. I can go wherever I like on this goddam planet. Do we run the world or not?"

No one took up the challenge of replying to Rump's question.

"Can someone show me Bangistan on a map?" continued the President.

"I believe that the CIA has finally found it," joked Zebriski. "How about it, O'Reilly?"

The President had been threatening Bangistan with hell and eternal damnation for the past three months, had promised several times to unleash a nuclear apocalypse on the tiny state, but no one seemed particularly surprised that Rump didn't actually know, or had forgotten, where it was located. They had grown used to such things.

O'Reilly got up, took a pointer stick and, after circling around the Caspian sea for a moment on the flip chart map, went north-east a little and brought it down firmly upon the recently discovered sixth Stan.

"Here you are, Mr. President. Goats, gas, uranium, a nuclear arsenal, many concentration camps and Ambassador Winkelmeier's current residence."

"It's pretty close to Russia and China, isn't it?" observed Rump, squinting at the flip chart.

"It has borders with both," O'Reilly confirmed.

"Why are *they* keeping so quiet about Akim and his threats to start a world war? Why are they leaving all the action to *me*?"

"According to CIA intelligence, they've decided to let us do the job for them," O'Reilly replied. "They want to keep their hands clean, while we either denuke Bangistan or take it off the map."

"Director O'Reilly is quite right, Sir," Ambassador Winkelmeier added. "The last thing Russia and China want is to face off against each other over Bangistan. Any move by either of them could be badly interpreted. They just want to see the back of Akim, actually. They both think he's a troublemaker who's ripping them off on gas supplies and prices."

"Not so dumb, those guys," mused Rump. "So, we have our hands free? I like it that way. Look, Ambassador, go back and tell Akim that I am going to do him a most incredible favor and come see him in … what was the name of the capital, again?"

"Petrobangorski, Sir."

"Jesus, just don't ever ask me to say it! Where was I? Yes,

tell him that I am ready to discuss openly and in friendship our options for an end to sanctions, to give full recognition to Bangistan, and to offer some very generous aid to his country. In exchange, he has to scrap his nuclear weapons programme and destroy his uranium enrichment plants. That's what they're called, isn't it, O'Reilly?"

"Yes, Sir, very good, Sir. But I still think it's very ill-advised for you to go to Bangistan, certainly at this stage. Much better Geneva or Vienna or somewhere like that. Agreeing to meet on his turf will look like we're kowtowing to this tinpot dictator. It'll be a huge propaganda victory for Akim and a real blow to the enormous esteem in which the world holds you."

President Rump assumed his most earnest mien, not unaffected by this obsequiousness, and replied sententiously: "Director O'Reilly. It lies on my shoulders to save the civilized world from war, and such considerations of my reputation are far beneath me in these circumstances. Though, personally, I think I will be given great credit for my courage, particularly compared to those disgraceful weaklings who sat previously in this chair. Yes! I'm going to Bangistan!" he said, slamming both his open hands down on the desk. "Fix it. The sooner the better."

And that was that. Everyone understood the meeting was over. As they all got up, Rump declared grandly, "'Peace in our time!' That's what I'll announce."

"I wouldn't, Sir, if I were you," said Zebriski. "It has an unhappy precedent."

The President wasn't listening any longer to anyone but himself, caught up in his ardent dream of winning a very special place in the history books. As the visitors quit the Oval Office, his last words boomed out behind them, *"Ich bin ein Bangistani!"*

Winkelmeier alone felt satisfied. He had been dealt his ace card – a summit in Petrobangorski. The presence of actors, the appearance and guaranteed victory of Akim's teenage daughter on The Voice, the erection of Akim's personal statue in Times Square (two demands the Ambassador had not dared to relay), even the promise of an immediate pull-out of US missiles from Europe, all these preconditions for a meeting with Rump would pale into insignificance with that gift. Akim knew that, thanks to the visit, he would become a legend in his lifetime and considerably enhance his international status, and these things would please him to the exclusion of anything else.

Holden, O'Reilly, Zebriski, together with their aides, who had hung at the back of the room scribbling and saying nothing, went off without enthusiasm to debrief each other and make sure that they all had the same story to tell of the President's decision. At the same time, each in his heart, though for quite different motives, swore that the Rump-Akim meeting must be thwarted at all costs, that it must never take place if they could help it. The US had been quite sufficiently humiliated already. None of the men were yet ready, however, to reveal their sentiments to the others. Careers were already short enough in this Presidency. It would be insane to destroy them prematurely by trusting someone.

That evening, as Ambassador Winkelmeier sat on the airplane, full of dread for the twenty-three-hour trip home to Akim Airport via Frankfurt, Istanbul, and Almaty, with a last, mercifully-short leg on Bangistan Airlines, he saw a breaking news flash appear on his telephone and read the first few lines: "East Bangistan mountains shake from underground thermonuclear explosion. US President tweets: 'Poisonous snake Akim breaks word on tests. Everything back on the table, including US preventive strikes. You're a loser, Hakim. Big time!'"

The Ambassador ordered a very large scotch from the hostess, took out his wallet, and looked tenderly at a photograph of dear Mrs. Winkelmeier. If all telecommunication connections between Bangistan and the outside world had not currently been blocked, he would have sent her a message of reassurance and his undying love. Instead, he took a deep swallow of his drink, reclined his seat a little and contemplated a long night and day ahead in the entrails of the air travel monster.

At the State Department, they just had time, minutes before its dispatch, to kill the upbeat media release announcing the President's brilliant diplomatic breakthrough in the Bangistan crisis.

CHAPTER 2

THE MAYOR'S BIG JOKE

Stephen Blakely held the basket of sliced baguette in the air as the waiter put a carafe of water in its place on the round, gilt-edged table. The Englishman then seized the salt, pepper, mustard and toothpick holder with his other hand to make way for the water tumblers.

The waiter hovered still, waving the wine bottle and other glasses suggestively and silently above them, obliging Ruth to make more space again by removing the just-arrived carafe and gesturing to her husband to do similarly with the tumblers. The bottle and wine glasses immediately occupied their places.

In his grand, final move, the waiter triumphantly deposited their plates in the empty areas delineated by their knives and forks and serviettes, before cheerfully announcing, "Bon appétit," putting his tray under his arm, and disappearing back into the café.

"Check mate, I reckon," Stephen told his wife.

"The man's a grandmaster," said Ruth.

They looked at each other across the table, the bread basket, the condiments, the carafe and the water tumblers dangling from their outstretched arms, and laughed gaily.

"I'll get a chair to put them on," said Stephen, rising and dragging an unoccupied stool from a nearby table with his foot, after gaining the consent of its occupants.

Every episode of sunshine, even in the depths of winter, drives the French out on to the terraces of their cafés, brasseries, bistrots and restaurants, the women aligned like sunflowers, their thankful, outstretched faces turning slowly with the sun's shifting rays. Today, in chilly, early spring, was no exception. There wasn't an empty table in sight in the three establishments bordering the little square.

"Do you think we'll ever have to go back?" asked Ruth between mouthfuls of her *omelette aux cèpes*. "To England, I mean," she added unnecessarily, lifting her face to absorb hungrily a little more warmth.

Stephen didn't reply and didn't need to. Happily, he and Ruth had that kind of privileged relationship in which questions generally contained their answers and, even when there were no answers, the sense of all that they had previously confided to each other and didn't need to repeat. He smiled, squeezed her hand, and eventually said: "You know I'll do my best." It was all she wanted or expected to hear.

"I really can't remember a week like this when you didn't get some urgent call or another," Ruth went on. "Isn't anything happening in the world, Mr. First Secretary? Are you not needed to resolve some crisis or other? To defend the interests of Her Majesty and her subjects somewhere? Haven't our dear American friends threatened anyone today?"

Stephen smiled. "As far as I'm concerned, the world can go to hell and the Yanks along with it as long as we can keep enjoying these few days here in peace and sunshine," he said gently. "All I know is that Rump and Akim are back to trading insults and comparing the size of their rockets. So, all is well in the global playground as long as that continues. In diplomatic spheres, the technical term for this is 'dialogue'."

No one had yet seen fit to inform Stephen of the previous day's thermonuclear test in East Bangistan.

It was on both their minds, but Ruth was the first to speak.

"A propos, you *did* see what I saw in the market, didn't

you?" They had exchanged glances at the time, but neither had said a word.

"The zucchini woman?" asked Stephen. Ruth nodded. "But I thought that I was perhaps hallucinating," he said. "Overwork, or something."

"No," smiled Ruth. "While we all thought he was playing golf in Florida, or drawing up plans to bomb Bangistan, Rump was actually selling *courgettes* in Gascony."

"What a truly incredible resemblance it was!" said Stephen. "It's a pity we didn't get a photograph."

"That's easily fixed. I'll wander back over to the market and you have your coffee and pay up. See you there." And off Ruth rushed.

The Luchère-Les-Bains market stall holders were closing up. Ruth skipped over the metal poles, colorful canvas sheets and crates of unsold produce now carpeting the ground and found her way to the zucchini stand, where a woman and a man were still at work.

"Elles sont magnifiques!" Ruth gushed to the old peasant couple, pointing at the huge, polished vegetables aligned still across their tables. The woman studiously ignored her, as the man asked, "Combien?" – how many of them?

Ruth spoke French well and quickly explained that she didn't, in fact, want to buy any of their most excellent zucchini today, but wondered if they would mind if she made a souvenir photograph. The man shrugged indifferently, which she took as a peculiarly Gallic consent, and turned away. Ruth whipped out her camera and clicked happily at the stall, the zucchini and, surreptitiously, the woman, before gracefully thanking them both and heading back to Stephen, who hadn't made it to the market but was still waiting to settle up with the chessmaster.

Ruth sat down and thrust the screen of her camera in front of her husband, running through her shots. "Remarkable, remarkable," said Stephen. "She's a dead ringer. Not only the face, of course, the blonde hair, the scowl, but she's about the same height and build as well. This will give the guys in the office a great laugh. Thank you sweetheart."

"She did look imperious, presidential, didn't she?" said Ruth. "Particularly standing there next to that little man. I wonder if they're a couple? I wouldn't fancy being in *his* shoes, poor fellow."

Stephen had now managed to pay the waiter and they got up to leave.

"What do you reckon, darling?" he asked Ruth. "A nap or a walkabout?"

"Let's explore Luchère-Les-Bains!" said his wife enthusiastically. Though Stephen yearned for his bed, he knew that, as usual, she was right to push them to action. It would be a pity to leave this nice little town undiscovered after they had come a couple of hundred of miles to find it. And so off they set. They never fussed about town maps, and certainly would never seek information on their telephones, and thus just wandered off towards *le fronton*, the pelota court, which they had seen on their way to the square and which, in the Basque region, was an even surer indication of the center of a town's life than the ubiquitous churches.

The couple ambled aimlessly in this way for two or three hours, admiring the flawless homogeneity of the white-washed stone and oak Basque houses, with their gently sloping terracotta-tiled roofs, both real and decorative half-timbered façades, and dark red and green stained wooden shutters. From time to time, they poked their noses into cobblestone courtyards, startling yawning cats.

The Blakelys were proud that they never did the things expected of foreigners in their forays into the depths of France. They felt, for these brief years at least, that they were at home, *chez eux,* and they loathed to be taken for tourists.

In the Basque region, this was often easier than elsewhere in the country. People didn't seem to make these distinctions; everyone appeared welcome and, if it was not the case, a natural discretion demanded that no fuss be made about it.

When they eventually tired of their walk, they made their way back to their little hotel along the empty streets. All the shops had been shut and they had hardly seen a soul all afternoon. Spain, just a few miles away, had apparently exported its excellent siesta here just over the border and their steps were accompanied by many grunts and snores escaping from behind the blinds of the houses.

"Feeling peckish, *mon amour*?" asked Stephen later, as they lay half-naked on the hotel room bed. After a short rest, a shower and an hour or so reading the novels they had brought with them, Stephen Blakely's mind had turned once more to perhaps his greatest pleasure in life. Eating and drinking.

Even though they found themselves in the land of the *double entendre*, Ruth resisted the bawdy retort that came instantly to her mind and instead said: "Yes, of course, quite peckish. Should I get tarted up?"

"Not especially, sweetheart. It seems to be a rather modest place, though I've read that we can eat very well. I'm getting famished even thinking about it. Just throw on the first clothes you find and let's go."

Entering *Chez Irène*, just two streets away, shortly afterwards, they were greeted warmly and loudly by the eponymous lady herself. "Soyez les bienvenus, mes chers petits!" proclaimed a fulsome, middle-aged woman wrapped in a vast, colorful apron and carrying a huge wooden spoon. "The soup!" she suddenly cried, pointing them towards a table with her ladle and rushing back into the kitchen.

They took the places that Irène had indicated, for the moment the only clients in the restaurant. She rapidly reappeared, bearing two glasses of a welcome apéritif which they drank while poring over the fare on the slate menu she had placed on a chair facing them. As they did so, other customers began to fill up the two dozen places in the establishment. Among them was a red-cheeked man wearing a black beret, who sat down at the table next to the Blakelys, embracing all present with his jovial, bilingual salutation, "Arratsalda on, Jaun-andreok! Bonsoir, Mesdames et Messieurs!"

"Bonsoir, Monsieur Le Maire!" came a chorus led by the *patronne*.

Mayor Lizarazu stroked his thick, drooping moustache at both ends and looked eagerly around him like one of those men who cannot for long remain silent if there is another human being within talking distance. This quality was no doubt one of the factors that had propelled him into the town hall thirty years before and kept bringing him back with the overwhelming support of the inhabitants. His curiosity soon alighted on the nice young strangers sitting just a couple of yards away from him. His keen ears caught that they were speaking not Euskara, not French either, but a foreign tongue …

"You are perhaps American?" said Lizarazu, leaning towards the Blakelys with a huge smile.

"No," said Ruth kindly. "We're English." "British, actually," Stephen corrected her. It may well be exactly the same thing for the French, he thought, but he had a professional duty to put them straight on this. Not even to mention that Ruth was, after all, Welsh, and he, half Scottish.

"Welcome to my little town," said the Mayor. "You like?"

Both Ruth and Stephen quickly lost themselves in gushing replies, swept along in a torrent of completely unjustified superlatives about the extraordinary beauty of Luchère-Les-Bains, the marvellous time they were having, the Mayor's wonderful command of English and the honor it was to meet him.

Ruth then felt it fit to add: "We didn't find the *Bains*, though, no baths, no trace of them, which was a slight disappointment. Maybe we could see them tomorrow before we leave."

"Heh, Irène!" Lizarazu suddenly shouted to the *patronne* across the restaurant as she delivered dishes to another table. "My American friends, they have been looking for *Les Bains!*"

Irène shrieked with laughter, setting off an uproarious concert of cackles and guffaws from the other clients as they tucked into their rich fish stew, their *ttoro*, and slugged back carafes of their local, *Irouléguy* wine.

"I think we're the entertainment tonight," said Stephen, joining in the general amusement and laughing too.

The Mayor eventually turned back to the British couple as the laughter faded away, beaming with pleasure and contentment as though he had just made the greatest joke of his life. He pulled his chair even closer to their table and whispered in a confidential tone: "You know why you never find them, the baths?" The Blakelys shook their heads and shrugged their shoulders. "It is because there are not any! They do not exist!" Lizarazu stared at one, then the other of them, and raised both his bushy eyebrows dramatically.

"But the name of your town? Luchère-*les-Bains*?" said a bewildered Ruth.

"I will tell you," said the Mayor, at the same time calling Irène to bring them all more drinks and to hold the stew a little longer. "You do not think that anyone would come here to our lost town if we were simply 'Luchère', do you? We are not on the road to or from anywhere, as you may have noticed. One day we were extremely *fatigué* of looking at each other and discussed – in this restaurant, in fact – how to bring new people here, a few Americans like you, for instance."

"British, *Monsieur Le Maire*, British," Stephen reminded him.

"Yes, yes, yes. British, American, *c'est la même chose*, non, the same thing?"

Stephen and Ruth just smiled. It certainly wasn't the occasion for a fight to defend the singular nature of the British identity.

The Mayor went on: "So, we changed our name, added 'Les Bains' – your 'baths' – a few years ago. It was my idea. Very clever, non? And who knows? The Romans could have built baths here, non? We have not dug very much. Anyhow, since then, the hotels have been full, Irène cannot keep up with business, the dogs and cats now have company when they watch the pelota games, and I can practice my English and meet charming young people like you Americans. But tell me, while looking for *Les Bains*, what *did* you see here? What did you like?"

"We adored the market," said Ruth. "The heaps of red pepper, the sausages, the terrines, the foie gras and confits, the legs of ham, the fantastic cheeses, the jams, so many kinds of fruit, the spectacular vegetables – above all the zucchini!"

"The zucchini?" Lizarazu enquired with interest. "This is American for *courgettes*, perhaps? Chez Marie-Pierre and Gaston, I suppose?"

"We don't know their names, I'm afraid," said Ruth. "But I have never seen such *courgettes*, such zucchini, in my life. One of them must have been a metre long!"

"At least," the Mayor concurred soberly. "In fact, if my memory is good, Marie-Pierre won the regional prize, the gold, with a beast who measured one metre and twenty centimetres! We are very proud of her."

"She wasn't very friendly, though, I must confess," said Ruth. "She completely ignored me, even though I was the only customer."

"Ah, but there is a reason for this," replied the Mayor. "It is very unusual, perhaps, but she does not speak French." He paused to let this extravagant information sink in.

"Only Basque, then?" enquired Stephen.

"Not even Basque," said the Mayor. "Or so she pretends, we are never quite sure. No, our Marie-Pierre she speaks only *Gascon*! Not many understand it around here, so she does not talk very much. Gaston has to translate for her when this is necessary to sell her courgettes. He is a good man, Gaston, quite *ad-mi-ra-ble*. We French love our martyrs, you know, and he is most *assurément* one such person."

"Now I must leave you, *hélas*," said Lizarazu. "The *ttoro necessitates* – good word, yes? – my full attention and concentration," he added, licking his moustache. "Otherwise, I will finish with the *langoustines* in my shirt."

At this, the Mayor moved back to his own table. Irène had also just set down their *ttoro* in front of them. They dived into the steaming bowls stuffed tight with fish heads, gambas, mussels, lobster. It was delicious, truly memorable.

Later, as they left the restaurant and bid goodnight to Irène and the remaining clients, the Blakelys passed by the Mayor, who was now regaling a large table of citizens with his tales, some, Stephen suspected, about naive *Estatubatuarrek* – Americans. He gave Lizarazu a friendly pat on the shoulder and told him: "*Bains* or no *bains*, we shall be back!" It was the polite thing to say, after all. What he did not know was that it would indeed be the case, and rather sooner than he expected. Indeed, Luchère-Les-Bains was destined to play an unusual and important rôle in the tale of Stephen Blakely's life, even though he would have to take the story, forever unspoken, with him to the grave.

The next morning, as they drove away from the town, heading a little deeper into the Pyrenees and vaguely towards Pau, they saw a giant grafitti, in English, on the side of a disaffected farm barn by the roadside: "Yankees go home! There are no Bains!" The paint looked quite fresh …

CHAPTER 3

THERE ARE TWO CONGOS

"Are you encrypted this morning, Sir?"

"I do have a bit of a hangover, Sally, it's true. Does it show that much? I've got to see the PM at twelve and you know how difficult it is to keep up a conversation with *her* if you don't have your wits about you. Many lags, you know. She just stares these days, most unsettling."

"Not you, Sir, I was asking whether your *telephone* was encrypted. Have you used the key today?"

"All this bloody secrecy," complained Ormrod. "You do it for me, won't you?"

"I can't, Sir, that's the point. I don't have the codes. Only you've got them. You mustn't let me know what they are."

Ormrod had been at the Foreign Office for barely three months and was tired already of all these rituals. At the Ministry of Digital, Culture, Media and Sport, no one had given a hoot about the way in which they conducted their business or, indeed, about whatever it was they were supposed to be doing there.

"What a fuss for nothing," said Ormrod. "Tell me, Sally, who on earth would want to listen in to my telephone calls?"

"Apart from the Russians, the Chinese and the Americans – not to mention the French, I can't imagine, Sir," said his assistant.

"All right, all right. Point taken. I must have the instructions here somewhere," he said, while rifling through his jacket pockets. "Anyone special likely to call?"

"Precisely, Sir. That's why I urge you to get the encryption sorted out right away. We've just been alerted that the American Secretary of State, Mr. Holden, will call at ten. That's in half an hour."

"It must be three or four a.m. over there," said Ormrod. "I wonder what that old bloodsucker wants with me in the middle of the night. It's true they say he never sleeps, too busy plotting the downfall of civilization."

"Right, if you'll fix the encryption, Sir, I'll put the call through as scheduled. Secretary Holden always calls on time, to the exact minute, you may remember."

"That's a nice dress you're wearing today, Sally," said Ormrod idly, as he watched her walk back to her adjacent office.

"Such things are not permissible to say in our times, Minister. You should know that. The new code of conduct in government and the civil service. You've read it of course? But thanks anyhow, I bought it this weekend." Her new boss was perfectly harmless in such matters, a real gentleman, and she was secretly pleased with his remark.

Codes, codes: to encrypt his telephone, to behave correctly with ladies, even to open the door of his own office. Ormrod was tired of them. And what on earth was he doing there in the Foreign Office anyhow? Problems, that's all they dealt with, problems day and night, problems seven days a week. Nothing he was ever called upon to do could be construed as constructive or positive, could be truly said to be advancing a worthy cause, improving the lot of humanity, for instance. At times this quite depressed him. Maybe he should have held on to the Ministry for Digital, Culture, Media and Sport, after all? That job had been great fun. But others had their plans for him apparently, plans cooked up at boozy lunches among party grandees and urged upon him as his duty to the nation and, if that wasn't good enough as an argument, his obligations to himself.

Ormrod's problem, the reason why no one would leave him in peace, was that he had been identified as some kind of political *wunderkind*, destined to rise effortlessly through the ranks of the party and government towards what no one doubted would one day be his triumphal entrance into 10 Downing Street. His secret, which few had pierced and which he had not himself even grasped, was that he had no ambition. This could take a man a long way in the world and even in politics, contrary to common belief. His manner also helped the case in his favor. He never contradicted anyone superior to him and, indeed, rarely those inferior in rank either. Cynical colleagues who had observed this, some of them irritated at his rapid ascension, thought it was a ploy. Yet it was only common politeness, that timeless English vice.

Yes, he mused, while continuing his search for the elusive encryption instructions, thrusting his hands repeatedly into the same four pockets of his jacket, he had greatly enjoyed his year at DCMS, as it was known. No one took the post seriously, of course, but the press and his colleagues had all assumed that his nomination was only part of the *plan*, that the party had put him there merely to test his mettle, uniquely to see if he indeed had the substance and personality to carry off a rôle in the Cabinet. As for the people, the public, they couldn't have cared less what he was supposed to be doing with his time there; they just liked him for the wit and ease he showed on all occasions and, particularly, when a guest on the television talk shows to which he was repeatedly invited.

Unlike the Foreign Office, a hideout for all manner of odd and dubious people, the DCMS staff had been most charming, young, enthusiastic, and relaxed, none of them appearing unduly overworked or stressed. He had endeared himself to them quickly and effortlessly with his good humor and informal style. He remembered the first meeting of personnel, when the senior staff had introduced themselves and a certain Penbroke had thrust himself forward as the 'Head of Digital'.

"Digital what?" asked the Minister maliciously.

"Digital, digital ... *stuff*, Sir," Penbroke replied awkwardly, to the laughter of his colleagues.

"You are not uncomfortable working for an *adjective*?" Ormrod continued. "Anyhow, if you're *Pen...broke*, I guess that digital is a good place to be." The staff had groaned with pleasure.

He had never in his life been to so many football and rugby matches, operas and concerts and art exhibitions, and could not believe that he was being paid for all this pleasure. The tickets and invitations just came pouring in to the Ministry and he took great care too to distribute them generously at all staff levels when a formal and 'official' presence was not required. New books also arrived by the cartload. Rather than having them archived or establishing a library, he invited staff to take them home if they fancied one or the other of them. This was probably against all rules of government, but the Minister didn't care in the slightest. Spreading culture was the objective, was it not?

He had enjoyed nothing quite so much as the encounters with his European counterparts. Few of them had been saddled with the 'digital *stuff*', or if they had, they were keeping quiet about it. Ormrod recalled endless, sumptuous lunches and dinners around the continent with his Greek, Italian, French and Spanish colleagues, and few of the much less amusing meetings, invariably around a tray of sandwiches, with the northerners, who took their jobs a little more seriously and appeared to consider Culture as a guilty indulgence at best. Yes, the Latins and the Greek were his favorites, all of them lively and cultivated and as relaxed as he was in their functions. Except, of course, when it came to heritage and thus matters of national pride and honor. His Greek friend Stavros Kamaras, for example, who regaled the other clients in the little restaurants to which he took Ormrod, with full-throated recitations of the poems of Nikos Kazantzakis between dishes. He asked Ormrod one day: 'You know the epitaph on his grave in Heraklion? I tell you. *'I hope for nothing. I fear nothing. I am free'*. You like?" Ormrod liked very much. He liked even to think that he could say as much of himself.

Unfortunately, Kamaras could not resist two things: trying just one more time to get back the Elgin Marbles ("I shall correct you, my friend Ormrod, again and again: they are the *Parthenon* Marbles and your Elgin was a mere thief and vandal, as the good Lord Byron himself pointed out"), and interjecting etymological reflections into Ormrod's conversation. Invariably, these bad habits manifested themselves as they opened their second bottle of ouzo.

"Taking the hypothesis," began Ormrod – "*Greek word*," broke in Kamaras – "that the Marbles" – "*Greek word*," he chimed in again – "were actually stolen, which we do not admit, I regretfully must tell you that Greece did not actually exist as a state at the time and that under international law we should have to give them back to Turkey, from whom we bought them. And they don't want them, as far as I know."

"Don't provoke me, Ormrod," said Kamaras, "with your Turk stories."

The Minister continued: "Our policy" – "*Greek word*" said Kamaras once more – "isn't likely to change, I fear. I am just the *messenger* – Greek word, I suppose?" ventured Ormrod. "No," said Kamaras, "Latin, though those Roman thieves probably took it from Greek, it's true."

Yes, those discussions about the restitution of cultural property had been no fun at all, thought Ormrod, looking at his watch and seeing that he had another fifteen minutes before the Secretary came on line. If it had been up to him he would have given absolutely everything back to whomever wanted it and could make a reasonable case that its acquisition had been questionable.

What had he achieved, though, at DCMS? He had wanted to change the rules for handball in soccer, but was politely informed by his staff that this was not exactly within the Ministry's remit or power but rather that of the 'Kingdom of FIFA', as the Head of Sport had put it, over which no one at all had any influence. Still, it remained an obsession with him, this very stupid idea that a referee could judge the *intentionality* of a gesture, judge that a footballer, perhaps with a death wish, had been so insane as to *deliberately* give away a penalty when there was no especial threat. Referees were not psychiatrists or mind readers, after all.

Various advances in digital rights management and the protection of intellectual property had been unjustly attributed to him, though, despite his protests that he understood nothing whatsoever about these questions. His endeavors to give credit to the staff who had actually resolved these complex dossiers were brushed aside as simply the manifestations of his legendary modesty.

No, his biggest and perhaps only personal coup, in his own mind, had been the Bayeux Tapestry, the celebrated woven account of the Norman invasion of the 11th century Kingdom of England. In that case he had succeeded where his Greek friend had failed. He *had* persuaded the French to return it … if only on loan, of course. It had cost him three trips to Paris and much eating and drinking too. A modest sacrifice, all in all. His French colleague, Charles Roche la Molière, had at first dismissed out of hand even the thought that this most precious testament to an English defeat at the hands of an army from France might cross the Channel, as it had indeed not done in almost a thousand years. "*If at all,*" he had insisted, since both countries claimed that it had been made in their lands and no one could settle the debate. France did not have *so many* such victories over which to gloat, he had to confess, and they were hanging on to the evidence of this one.

Little by little, however, Roche la Molière had softened his stance. It was, after all, perhaps *really* made in England, judging by the awfully clumsy quality of the needlework, he said with a pernicious smile on the occasion of their second dinner discussion. Such *lack of artistry* was not French at all.

And then, finally, during their last dinner, on Ormrod's invitation and at the British Embassy, Roche la Molière had announced the good news.

"This matter of the Tapestry, it has been discussed in very, *very* high places! In all its beneficence, France has decided that you can borrow it for a little while."

"That's fantastic, most splendid!" gushed Ormrod. "I'm so grateful for all your efforts, *mon ami*."

"There is a condition, though," the Frenchman added. "Before you return our Tapestry, you must sew back the missing piece, the one you stole, the final *titulus* you are hiding, in the Tower of London perhaps? '*Et fuga verterunt Angli*'. And the English turn in flight! They run away from the fight!" They had both laughed their heads off about that and called for more cognac and long into the night had celebrated this historic new stage in the Entente Cordiale between their nations.

"Secretary Holden on one, Sir," came Sally's voice from the loudspeaker.

"Good morning, Ormrod."

"Good morning, Mr. Secretary. It's a trifle late – or early – for you, isn't it?"

"This is rather embarrassing," began Holden, ignoring

Ormrod's question. "We got it wrong on Bangistan, pulled the trigger too quickly. You'll see it on the news later, but I wanted you to hear it first. It wasn't a nuclear test, all that shaking in the mountains, but an earthquake. The Chinese told us. We trust them on this. They've been into seismology for four thousand years, you know."

"Indeed," said the Minister. "But how on earth did you make the mistake?"

Holden didn't much like Ormrod's supercilious English tone but nevertheless replied: "It was Fox News. They reported it after a tip off from NASA. The President happened to be watching and the tweet was gone before we had any confirmation. There'll be a retraction in a couple of hours. We'll say Bangistan denies the test, no one will believe them, and we'll be in the clear. It'll all be forgotten by tomorrow."

"But what about Akim? How has he taken to being called … what was it … a snake?"

"He fired back some abuse questioning the President's mental condition, nothing serious or new."

"And now?"

"Our Ambassador will be back in Petrobangorski later today and will have to go and crawl a bit. He's good at crawling, really among the best. He'll smooth things over."

"Fine, fine," said Ormrod. "It's awfully kind of you to let me know this personally, Holden. I'm seeing the Prime Minister in a few hours and will brief her too."

"Just one more thing I should tell you, Minister. President Rump, against my advice, has decided to go personally to Bangistan to try and resolve the whole business once and for all. Details in a few days, hopefully."

"Good Lord."

Secretary Holden mumbled "Yes, Good Lord" and hung up without so much as a 'goodbye'.

Ormrod had never even heard of Bangistan before joining the Foreign Office. It was not at that time in the news headlines, it's true. The country had risen to international prominence only since Rump had two months earlier begun, for obscure reasons, to provoke and threaten it. On the urging of the belligerent Holden, said some; on the advice of his political strategists, anxious to take attention away from domestic problems, proposed others.

The country had not been mentioned at all during Ormrod's first briefings at the Foreign Office, even though these sessions were intended to initiate him in the complexities of the world and its nations. Inheriting a new Minister, the civil servants were always most anxious to ensure that he or she should have a minimal knowledge of what was where and why and what they were talking about. They did not want their Nambias.

Ormrod wished he had been more studious about geography at school; he felt as though he didn't know the world at all when actually put to the test. The experts who ran the briefings were trained, of course, not to embarrass senior members of the government and he had never had to admit to any of his ignorance. There were two Congos? He had always suspected it. The republic of Dominica was not the same place as the Dominican Republic? Who could possibly have confused them? The first was to be found in the Lesser Antilles and the second in the Greater; it went without saying. He had even successfully hidden his perplexity about the Guineas, all four (or was it five?) of them: Equatorial Guinea, the People's Revolutionary Republic of Guinea, Guinea-Bissau and New Guinea, which just to confuse matters further, comprised both Papua New Guinea and Western New Guinea (the first of which was independent, the other ruled by Indonesia, and together, the civil servants told him, was the home of one thousand and seventy-three languages).

He still had trouble spelling Kyrgyzstan, but then who didn't?

The second briefing had been more political and *strategic*. This time, the maps on the slide show had sought, using different colors, to distinguish between 'Friendly' and 'Unfriendly' nations. In their attitude and intentions towards the United Kingdom, naturally. The Friendlies were rose-colored, the Unfriendlies, brown.

"It was a lot simpler when it was all red and British," said Ormrod complacently, to many grunts of approval and mutterings about Empire and the never-setting sun. "But tell me, what about those countries which are neither rose nor brown? Just white."

"Frankly, Sir? Those are countries to which we don't pay much attention," said the head expert. "They may be Friendly or Unfriendly, of course, but we don't really care very much; they are in no way key to British interests and are doubtless just after our money."

His third introductory briefing had been about war, or 'ongoing armed situations', as the experts had put it. These were neatly divided into categories: major wars, minor wars, conflicts, skirmishes and clashes, according to the level of their 'cumulative fatalities', as one expert had put it delicately. A lot of people are dying whatever you call it, thought Ormrod, who discovered that on any given day, people were being murdered for ideas, religions and ethnic differences in more than three dozen 'situations'.

Among the nations that the Foreign Office had at that time consigned to the United Kingdom's neither Friendly nor Unfriendly cartographic indifference was Bangistan. In the past two months, all the slides had rapidly been reworked, of course. Bangistan was now most decidedly worth a color, and it was brown. President Hakim Akim had, after all, called the Prime Minister a donkey and described Her

Majesty the Queen as an 'American lackey'. To attack the PM was fair game, thought the Foreign Office, but the Queen was completely out of bounds. The matter had become serious.

Yes, Ormrod reminded himself, Bangistan was today a 'country we care about' and, incontestably, 'Unfriendly'. It could also now be categorized as a potential agent of a most terrible and major conflict, brought on by repeated verbal skirmishes. Only President Rump could change any of this, it appeared, particularly since he had largely created the crisis in the first place.

CHAPTER 4

THE PPDRB

The People's Popular Democratic Republic of Bangistan had none of the qualities that its grandiloquent name suggested.

It was not governed by or for its People and the founders had certainly never had the intention that it should be. It was, rather, the exclusive, private domain of the Akim family, now in its fifth generation of rule under one flag or another.

To whom it might be Popular was unclear. Of Democracy, there was little trace, outside of elections for a phantom Parliament every seven years. These plebiscites were nevertheless great triumphs for the ruling Akimist party, which alone was permitted to have contenders. Voting was mandatory and took place without privacy and in front of nervous members of the security police. One hundred percent of the population of Bangistan backed the regime's candidates. Some western apologists, for the most part political scientists and minor politicians, even claimed to take this statistic seriously, out of a penchant for underdogs, an unavowed hatred of universal suffrage, or plain stupidity.

As far as the Presidency was concerned, Akim had greatly simplified matters. He had organized one direct election fifteen years earlier, after the death of his father. To the question, "Do you agree that President Akim should be elected for life?," only one option had been proposed on the ballot paper: 'Yes'.

No more than any other modern dictators did the nepotistic Akims admit the nation's incontestable totalitarian reality or have the courage to call a spade a spade and a dictatorship a dictatorship. Thus it was that the family had identified the country, mainly for internal consumption and despite all the evidence, as a 'Republic'.

Bangistan had until the early 1990s been a part of the Soviet Union and good Moscow loyalists. The Communist Party of Bangistan, led by Comrade Hassan Akim and his father before him, de facto rulers of the country even under socialism, had repressed and enchained their long-suffering people as well as anybody in the Soviet family of nations and, indeed, with a certain additional zeal that made them very popular in the Central Committee. Cruelty and a total lack of regard for life – other people's, that is – apparently ran in the family veins. Hakim Akim was made of the same stuff as his predecessors and was pleased to carry on the tradition of tyranny and subjugation long after communism per se had disappeared. The citizens of this far-flung ex-Soviet state had seen no difference or change at all when the Berlin Wall had fallen; indeed, it was an event that had not even reached their ears. They remained in crass poverty and ignorance and barely knew that the outside world existed.

In this way, for two and a half decades after the Soviet collapse, Bangistan and its ruling dynasty had lived in splendid isolation. No one came into the country and no one went out. With the exception, that is, of the traffickers of uranium and of nuclear warheads who plied their trade in the region, and a handful of foreign academics who saw an opportunity to feed at the tyrant's trough in exchange for a few complacent papers here and there in obscure political magazines read only by other academics. Nobody who mattered knew about the warheads or the uranium or, if they had ever done, had forgotten them. Telephones and computers were, of course, illegal, except for members of the Akim family and those who served them; the country was thus impervious to,

and protected against, the nefarious influence of information.

In the deliquescent months and years following the
breakup of the USSR, everyone in a position to do so had
grabbed what he could as quietly as possible. The Akims
were no exception. They found themselves alone with an immense stockpile of nuclear weapons that had been placed in
their keeping twenty years earlier during a serious Soviet rift
with China along their joint border. Every day, the Akims expected the Russian Federation to ask for their bombs back.
The call had never come. The uranium mines were, of course,
theirs for keeps since they couldn't, after all, be moved. And
a very good source of income they proved to be, too. Together with the gas, of which both China and Russia bought
large quantities, these natural resources had made the Akim
family incredibly rich.

Needless to say, Bangistan did not belong to the United
Nations or to any other global or even regional organization.
It had no trading pacts or other formal agreements with anybody. This isolationism had enabled Bangistan, deliberately
or otherwise, to be practically ignored by the international
community, something it judged to be of considerable benefit. Most importantly, everyone kept their noses out of its
business.

All was thus well and tranquil for the rulers of Bangistan,
a resolute non-member of any collective organization of men
and peoples, with no internal or external opposition to speak
of. It could indeed have remained that way for the rest of
time. Then the Akims had made their fatal move. They had
joined Twitter.

CHAPTER 5

AKIM GETS HIS MOVIES

It reminded the Ambassador, an enthusiastic soccer fan, of the endless walk that players have to make from the half-line when their turn comes in a decisive penalty shootout after a drawn match. The distance between the huge, golden doors that opened into Hakim Akim's office and the desk at which the President sat, must have been a full sixty yards.

As Winkelmeier advanced slowly and in trepidation across this interminable space, while the President ostentatiously busied himself with his papers, a small, elderly woman appeared from a side door and, almost bent in two, shuffled her way in the same direction, heading him off just before his final destination. Akim growled something.

"Great Leader he say stick your big fat ass there," she translated, indicating the chair in front of Akim's bureau.

Winkelmeier did as he was told and began to stutter his carefully prepared, humble apologies for the most unfortunate occurrences of the last twenty-four hours …

Not yet looking up at him, Akim interrupted the Ambassador with another barked phrase.

"Great Leader he say shut it, he gonna do the talkin'," the old lady said while sitting down next to him.

Where on earth did she learn to speak like that? the Ambassador wondered. Perhaps she has also been watching Akim's gangster movies? But surely that wouldn't be allowed for such a lowly person as an interpreter?

Finally, Akim deigned to look at him, anger in his clouded, black eyes, and launched into a furious tirade, interrupted from time to time only by the bold translator, who conveyed the essence of his spleen.

"That total shit on test, you know, you know Winkelmeier? What that stupid pig Rump have in place brains? Who he think he dealing with? What point of test, if he not told by us? Next time we test rocket we test for real in Florida Disneyland. You see. No more Donald Duck! Mickey Mouse ...," and here she completed Akim's idea with a finger swept across her throat.

The President quickly got tired of his violent diatribe and mumbled a few more words to the woman.

"Great Leader he say 'what you bring, Winkelmeier?'"

The chastened Ambassador promised that he had brought important, good news from Washington.

"No, no," said the interpreter. "Great Leader mean what movies? You bring movies, no?"

Winkelmeier had indeed done as bidden and as usual on his trips to Washington. He opened his briefcase, brought out a dozen DVDs, all the latest hoodlum and crime films, and laid the pile on Akim's desk. "A gift from the President," he lied.

Akim smiled for the first time that morning, shuffling through the lurid covers and putting one or two aside as worthy of his especial attention.

"So, what else?" asked the woman, though the President had said nothing.

"I have very good news for you, Sir," said the Ambassador, gaining in confidence. "As a mark of his esteem for you and for Bangistan, and in view of the necessity for a major gesture after our most unfortunate mistake yesterday, President Rump has instructed me to inform you that he has most exceptionally decided to accept your kind invitation to come here to Petrobangorski to further the current efforts to create a new era of friendship and brotherhood and peace between our two great nations."

He did not understand how this magnificent speech could be conveyed in only four or five words by the old woman, but that was clearly all he was getting. Akim's reaction swept all his doubts away. The President got up, came round his desk, plucked the Ambassador from his chair, and while hugging him closely smacked great, wet kisses on both his cheeks. He then whispered: "I love you, Winkelmeier." They were the only words he knew in English and they made the Ambassador very happy.

Releasing Winkelmeier from his embrace, Akim grabbed the interpreter around the waist, planted his lips on the top of her head, and swept her away in a waltz, singing a traditional Bangistani folk song at the top of his voice.

The old lady shouted back at Winkelmeier across the room: "Great Leader he say you come back Friday tell him what Rump give him for peace."

"Of course, most willingly," boomed the Ambassador above Akim's rich and rather pleasant baritone. "Please tell the Great Leader I will also inform His Excellency what we request from Bangistan in return."

She ignored this remark and pointed at the door. Winkelmeier took the hint and strode back out, the great golden doors opening magically in front of him. After marching, accompanied by two sinister, wax-faced armed soldiers, the mile or two towards the street, along endless, silent, deserted corridors, he found himself back out in the sunshine. On the steps of the Presidential Palace, he walked straight into Yogi Akim, who appeared to have been waiting for him.

"Mr. Ambassador! Welcome home!" declared Akim warmly, seizing him with both hands, which Winkelmeier shook reluctantly, remembering, as always, that they were said to be used regularly to beat and occasionally to strangle unfortunate inhabitants of the regime's prisons.

"How is the lovely Mrs. Winkelmeier? My wife says that she is neglecting her," he smiled.

"Actually," said the Ambassador, "I'm on my way home to see her right now. I came here directly from the airport to deliver President Rump's message."

Yogi Akim laughed. "You have to explain very big screw up, perhaps? But what did you say? What's *the deal*, as you Americans put it? Where are we in all this *most* unfortunate business?"

"I'm sorry, Mr. Akim, I can't tell you. You'll have to hear it directly from your brother, I'm afraid."

Akim smiled again, his golden teeth glinting in the sunlight. "My brother don't trust me, Winkelmeier, you know that. He won't tell me nothing."

"Far be it from me to suggest subterfuge, Mr. Akim, something in which you of course excel, but why don't you invite the interpreter, that old lady, in for a chat? I'm sure that with the right incentives she could be persuaded to share our discussions with you. I simply cannot."

"That 'old lady', Winkelmeier, is my esteemed mother, Hakim's too. She does not like you, by the way, ever since you were overheard to refer to me as a *son-of-a-bitch* to one of your foreign colleagues. We have ears everywhere, Ambassador. You should be more careful."

And with that, Akim skipped gaily down the Palace steps and disappeared into his sleek, black Lincoln Continental limousine. Winkelmeier got into his own, rather more modest, car and instructed the Embassy chauffeur to take him home. Mrs. Winkelmeier had promised him roast goat head for dinner. After initial skepticism, he had come to adore it.

CHAPTER 6

AN ILLUMINATION IN LOURDES

Where others, feverish with hope, saw healing and, perhaps, impending miracles, the Blakelys perceived nothing but despair and tragedy.

"Do you think we'll see an apparition?" Ruth asked optimistically.

"Ronald Rump selling zucchini in Luchère-*sans*-Bains is quite enough in the way of supernatural phenomena for one trip," said Stephen.

They had joined the back of an immense queue of the infirmed, a walking hospital, heading for the grotto; a moving forest of crutches, canes, wheelchairs, stretchers; the lame leading the blind; the crippled leading the paralysed; the tormented shepherding the insane; countless diseased bodies and souls staggering towards an improbable salvation, accompanied by a swarm of idle, healthy tourists, many unpacking foil-wrapped lunches for their long wait.

"Don't you feel uncomfortable, out of place?" asked Stephen. "All this sickness, the combined stench of sandwiches and pestilence, the throes of death. I'm not sure that I can stand it, personally. Perhaps some of these people are infectious."

"Don't be so cruel, so mean!" protested Ruth, with a guilty giggle. She knew very well when her husband wanted to quit; she didn't need him to tell her directly. She had insisted that they should push on to Lourdes from Pau, but realized now that she had made a mistake. She grasped his hand and pulled him away, back towards the entrance to the sanctuary. He didn't protest.

"Sorry, my darling," said Stephen sheepishly. "I really felt ill at ease. I know you wanted to see it all. Why don't you go back on your own? I'll go and have a drink."

"I'm not quitting *you*, you miserable old bastard," said Ruth kindly.

"You know what I'd like to do?" said Stephen, as they walked back down the town's main street, zigzagging between stalls stacked high with Virgin Mary statuettes, religious Russian dolls, keyrings, ashtrays, flasks of grotto water, candles, paintings, snow globes, any imaginable trinket to which one might affix a representation of the Madonna. "I'd like to take a sledgehammer and smash all this to pieces. Such godless people these merchants, it's unbearable."

"Please restrain your desire to cleanse the temple for a few more minutes, darling," said Ruth. "Let's get out of town and be on our way. We can find a restaurant on the road. Any news on Bangistan, by the way? You haven't mentioned it today."

Stephen, warming up to his denunciation of the whole Lourdes charade, continued: "Do you know how many *allegedly* miraculous healings there have been at that grotto in the last one hundred and sixty years? I looked it up. Seventy at last count. About half the number of sick pilgrims who have been killed in road accidents on the way here to be cured." And after a pause: "I made up that last figure, but it's probably far short of reality."

When Stephen didn't approve of something, he went to great lengths to explain and justify his opinions. Many people found this very tedious; for Ruth it was immensely endearing. Her husband was a true man of conviction, an idealist and, even better than this, he was an optimist. He hated cynics and defeatists and believed deeply that his role in life was to try and improve the lot of his fellow humans. She loved him deeply for all this.

"Yes, *mon chéri*, I suppose you're right," said Ruth diplomatically. "But I see no harm in faith, in belief. You can't begrudge giving people some hope and solace, even if others try and empty their pockets while selling them their dreams."

"Vultures! Thieves! All of you!" shouted Stephen in a parting curse to the shopkeepers as they left the street, passing through the middle of a dense group of German tourists heading for the sanctuary. Several of the visitors bowed their heads or looked away; one man nudged his companion, pointed his finger at his temple and twirled it.

"I'm taking him back to the asylum," Ruth told the group loudly and reassuringly. "*Zum Krankenhaus!*" she ventured. Many nodded and smiled with pity and compassion.

Once round the corner and out of sight, they ran gaily towards the car park. "So, I'm mad, am I?" asked Stephen, grabbing Ruth tightly and hugging her. "Madly in love with you, that I'll admit."

"I was asking about Bangistan," Ruth reminded him once they were back on the road.

"Yes, I'm sorry. Now we can breathe fresh air again, I'll tell you. We procured a copy of the American Ambassador's report on his new meeting with Akim. It seems that things have been smoothened out for the moment. We didn't understand everything – the note said that Akim had 'loved the DVDs', which we think is a coded message that the Americans aren't sharing with us – but it's clear that everything is back on track."

"And what is it, the track?"

"As things stand, barring any actual new bomb tests or

missile launches, Rump will go to Petrobangorski directly from the Versailles G7. This means, in theory at least, that we'll all get a chance to try and influence him on the deal that he proposes to make with Akim."

"He's going, *in person*, to Bangistan? You didn't tell me that."

"Sorry, my love. I thought I had. Things are moving so quickly it's difficult to keep up."

"How astonishing, anyhow. As for influence, I thought he never listened to anybody," said Ruth.

"It's true the Prime Minister doesn't seem to have much, if any, pull on him, despite our so-called special relationship. I'm not sure that any of the others do either. But we do have to try."

"And where do you come in, my love?"

"It appears I'll get the job of coordinating whatever discussions we might have on Bangistan at Versailles. My old pal Ormrod apparently insisted to Sir Edmund that I should be our lead man on this. That was nice of him, wasn't it? I have to call him when we get back to discuss tactics."

"And what does Ambassador Edmund Pickering think about that? Isn't he irritated that Ormrod should be designating people from the Embassy's own staff?"

"Oh, he doesn't care in the slightest. One less thing for him to worry about. He's gone completely native now, you know, ever since his wife went back to England to prepare their return at the end of the year. He's fallen in love with Culture, suddenly. Spends most of his time wining and dining the literati and smooching with actresses."

"*Not* a good example to follow when you become Ambassador, my dear."

Stephen smiled.

"In fact, it was the Bayeux Tapestry coup that pushed him over the edge. Good old Ormrod very typically eclipsed his own rôle and gave Pickering all the credit. The Ambassador is now a triumph in London – he even got a call of thanks from the Queen.

"Anyhow, I'm going to have dinner with Schurz next week to see if we can't cook up something together," he added. "He's in charge of America's G7 preparations on the ground here."

"Scott? I *do* like him," said Ruth. "What does *he* feel about the whole crisis?"

"He's pulling his hair out with everybody else. All of them – us, as well, of course – are scared that Rump has become completely uncontrollable. I don't think *anyone* wants him to go to Bangistan. We're all terrified that he'll either give away too much, or that he'll storm out of the talks and declare war."

"Do you know something, Ruth?" asked Stephen suddenly, after they had been driving a while. "I've just had *the* most extraordinary illumination, a real revelation. I think I may have stumbled on an idea how to prevent all this, how to ensure that there's peace."

Ruth waited for him to tell her more, but he remained silent. He was a man who liked to think things through before settling on an idea or expressing an opinion, and she respected this. He would say what he had to say if and when the moment was right. She just lent over and kissed him on the cheek, and said:

"Perhaps Our Lady of Lourdes got to your case after all."

CHAPTER 7

HOW THE CRISIS BEGAN

Apart from Hakim Akim, only one living soul in Bangistan knew the most secret of the nation's many secrets.

This man was Yogi Akim. His knowledge of the secret was at the same time his passport to life and, one day but not for now – as these things went in Bangistan – it would more than likely be his passport to a precocious demise.

Yogi Akim's indelible sin was to have been personally responsible, in more ways than one, for instigating the chain of events that had led the secret to exist. For this, he had earned the undying hatred of his Great Leader of a brother. And that was not a very healthy situation to be in, as many deceased people had discovered. Yogi Akim laughed it all off, but nevertheless carried a machine gun and a crate of grenades in his limousine, two pistols under his jacket, and a knife in each of his crocodile leather boots. He also took great care to remunerate exceptionally well the members of his personal guard, who were as heavily armed as he and had every interest, financially speaking, in keeping him alive as long as possible.

It had all begun four months earlier with Henry Tate's trip to Zurich. Acutely suspicious and paranoid in nature – it was the basis of his most successful career as head of the Bangistani security police, one of his many official functions – Yogi Akim took great care to cover his tracks, most especially on the rare occasions he left the country. He travelled incognito, under this or that fake identity, with the most beautifully forged documents that the legendary Bangistani craftsmen could produce. Among his assumed names, Tate was his favorite. It had about it a certain *snap*, a certain short, sharp brutality, quite in keeping with its bearer's personality.

The Swiss have always been as neutral about the colour of money as they have endeavored to be about everything else. In the case of the money put into their good care by the Akims, it had a blood-red hue and was the fruit of confiscation, pillage, murder, and extortion through blackmail and torture. Together, naturally, with simple theft, during sham campaigns against corruption inspired by the excellent example of their Chinese and Russian neighbors. They had robbed widely and well, throughout the nation, and accumulated vast wealth, as all self-respecting authoritarian leaders must do if they are to be taken seriously and want to be ranked in Forbes magazine.

Faced with increasing international pressure, the Swiss had said repeatedly, with sombre, straight faces and their best impersonations of remorse, that they would clean up their act and be more attentive to the origin of the funds deposited in their banks. They had nevertheless stopped short of asking anyone to take their money back and had sent emissaries from time to time to reassure the Akims and other kleptomaniac dictators that their fortunes were quite safe. The Akims didn't trust Swiss bankers any more than they trusted anyone else and thought it best to check that their money was indeed still there where they had put it.

This is why Henry Tate came to Zurich, where he intended also to verify whether the excellent reputation of the local bordellos was justified. The Swiss, who were on the whole fine, upstanding people, were completely neutral also about the exploitation of women for sex, as long as the girls continued to arrive fresh from Budapest, Bangkok, Moscow and Kiev, and did not originate in Basel, Winterthur or Neuchatel, which would have greatly upset their neutral Helvetic consciences.

After a grueling day in the Akims' private vault at their bank in Bahnhofstrasse, where he had counted and re-counted the nine hundred and sixty-five gold bars, the five dozen, yard-high piles of American dollars, and countless chests of diamonds and other precious stones, biting one or other from time to time with his gold teeth to make sure they had not been replaced by glass counterfeits, Yogi headed off for some rest and recreation at the Edelweiss Boom Boom Club.

He needed a good whipping, and that's what he got. Olga was a virtuoso and she set about his body with enthusiasm, flaying his buttocks and other sensitive parts of his anatomy until they began to smart, shouting crude insults at him in three or four languages, and pressing the heels of her black stiletto boots hard into his back.

Later, sitting together over a beer at the bar, Yogi asked her where she found her tremendous energy and strength for flogging and torture.

"I imagine you are Putin," she said simply.

"Vladimir? He is practically my brother!" boasted Yogi groundlessly.

They had dined and had enjoyed each other's company, to the degree that Yogi thought perhaps he had again fallen in love, as he did regularly. He proposed to Olga that they should keep in touch, with the perspective that she might even come to Petrobangorski from time to time to whip him. Olga thought this was perhaps premature, and invited him instead to follow her on Twitter.

"Twit what?" asked Yogi, who did not at all catch her meaning.

To Olga's astonishment – she thought, at first, that he was joking – Yogi had never heard of Twitter. Laughing at him, she asked whether the Internet did not perhaps exist in his obscure country?

"Yes and no," said Yogi. "We have not developed our own, but we find ways to get into it through Russia when we need to. Which is not very often and for me, personally, never. But tell me about this 'Twitter' where I can follow you, my dear."

Olga explained as best she could that absolutely everyone in the world frequented this place where they could share information about themselves and their tastes, ask silly questions, and express their opinions on anything that crossed their minds. Pop stars, kings and queens, models, actors, presidents, sportsmen, politicians, terrorists, desperate authors, sado-masochistic escort girls like her ...

"I follow Pope Francisco," said Olga, a most religious girl, while crossing herself. "On Instagram too." Yogi had not heard of that either but, fearing further ridicule, kept this to himself.

"Would you show me?" he asked her.

"Who should I look for?"

"You really mean *everybody* is there?"

Olga nodded and got out her smartphone.

"Well, how about Xi Jinping? Try it: X-i, space, J-i-n-p-i-n-g."

Olga found that there were many accounts for the Chinese President, perhaps not all of them legitimate, but that certainly wasn't *her* problem. She opened one at random and read Xi's first tweet out loud:

"'What is it about dictatorship that you don't understand?'"

"Good question!" said Yogi. "Now try Putin."

"'My thoughts and prayers are with the Ukrainian people. At least what's left of them'."

"Excellent," said Yogi. "I will have much fun with this, I think."

He thought about inviting Olga upstairs again to wrap up the day with another good beating, but instead decided to return to his hotel to play a little more with this amazing toy that connected him instantly to all the world's big shots.

Before they each went their way, Olga gave Yogi a brief lesson in how to use Twitter, how to register, choose a *handle*, how to use *hashtags*, make specific word searches and so on. He gave her a gigantic tip on top of the house's whipping tariff for her troubles.

*

I wonder if anyone ever talked about Bangistan on this Twitter thing, Yogi Akim conjectured as he settled in for the evening in his Baur au Lac suite, a bowl of caviar at his side and two bottles of *Clos d'Ambonnay*, his favorite champagne, on ice.

He opened the hotel's computer on his bureau, found his way to the Twitter site, and read the instructions on how to register. He would have to come up with a *handle* in order to get an account? I'd better do it in Hakim's name, he thought. My brother would never forgive me if he were not Bangistan's first ever member of this incredible club.

After thinking it over for a few moments, he found it: "@bestdespot". Yes, that was good, snappy; Hakim would like that.

When he was all set, Yogi Akim launched a word search for 'Bangistan'. He fell instantly upon a page of very ugly and obscene insults from a group of so-called 'Bangistani Exiles For Freedom' that he had never heard of. He made a mental note to deal appropriately with these renegades at another time. The arms of Bangistani security agents were very long, after all, and on occasion could reach out to 'exiles' too.

He could find only one other reference to his country, but it shook him profoundly. It was a tweet sent ... by the President of the United States of America! Ronald Rump himself! He could hardly believe his eyes. Even less so when he read the text:

"Bangistan, Bangistan. You're dead!" *

It was at that precise moment that the die was cast for one of the most serious crises in recent world history…

*

Henry Tate cut short, with regret, his Zurich interlude and took the first plane homeward the following morning.

Arriving many hours later in Petrobangorski, he went straight to the Presidential Palace and recounted everything he had learned to his brother. Yogi had to explain the whole Twitter business three times before Hakim really understood what he was talking about, but it finally sank in. The President was as astonished, as furious and as horrified about Rump's tweet as his brother had been.

---

* *Editor's Note: Much later, when everyone had forgotten the origin of the Bangistan crisis, or didn't care any longer,* The New York Times *reported that President Rump had in fact slipped up while celebrating the gunning down of a radical Islamic terrorist, a Pakistani national on the run from the police, in a manhunt that had gripped the American nation. At the time, it was assumed that Rump had made a clever little joke embracing the terrorist's death with the friction between the US and Islamabad over the alleged recruitment of ISIS fighters in Pakistan. The gunman had been baiting the President for several days with insulting tweets (the FBI had asked Twitter to continue to publish them in an effort to locate him), much to the joy of other subscribers. The* Times *revealed that in response to the bloody conclusion of the police chase, and with his inimitable sense of repartee, Rump had in fact typed 'Bang, Bang, you're dead!' Predictive software had done the rest. After the Nambia fiasco, White House staff had extended the President's text predictions to include all the nations of the world, just to make sure that the country that flew out of his telephone actually existed. Of such small blunders too, history is often made.*

The Great Leader was known for his decisiveness, his ability to rapidly sum up a situation and take action. He immediately ordered that a team of computer scientists should be formed and that they should get working on connecting him permanently to Twitter. Best to go through China at first, he suggested; they were more competent than the Russians in such matters. With great deference, the head of the computer team informed him that the Great Leader was, as always, quite right, and that Chinese telecommunications were, indeed, superior, but that, unfortunately, Beijing had banned and blocked Twitter, as it had just about every other social network. They would thus have to continue to go through Russia until they could create their own, Bangistani, infrastructure. Hakim acquiesced. He knew everything about censorship and its merits, but nothing about science.

Alongside the computer specialists, Hakim also ordered the creation of team of translators, who installed themselves as best they could in two or three of the four hundred and fifty empty rooms in the Palace, near to the Great Leader's office. They were ordered to stay there day and night at the beck and call of the President. Food was brought in to them, but they had to sleep on the floor. None of this was unusual in Bangistan.

The war of words began.

Hakim Akim started modestly, sending off a string of taunts and insults about the American President's fake golf handicap, his IQ, the amount he paid women to sleep with him ("Come to Bangistan, here it's free!" he mocked one time), and the 'piddling' amount of Rump's personal fortune when compared to "Putin, Xi – and me, of course!"

Yogi, the pioneer of Twitter in Bangistan, quietly bolstered Hakim's traffic scores, submerging his messages in 'likes' and 'retweets' (something the computer team fixed easily) and, since Great Leaders are nothing without followers, making very sure to build a huge audience for his sacred words.

Much to Yogi's surprise, @bestdespot soon took on a life of its own and became hugely popular. The reactions to his brother's posts were overwhelmingly positive, particularly those from America. "Awesome," "Right on, dude!," "You're amazing," "Just ADORE your handle!," "You can Bangistan me anytime, babe!" and other panegyrics flooded the notifications. Yes, some were negative, but these were generally nonsense. The most frequent insult was "Fucking liberal!," which Yogi found incomprehensible as a description of the family's political philosophy.

Monitoring personnel at the National Security Agency were quick to spot Akim's tweets. Their superiors passed on the information to the CIA and the news went, very rapidly, all the way up to Director Dan O'Reilly. A foreign head of state was mocking America and, personally, the President. It was a serious matter.

O'Reilly went to see Rump to inform him what had been going on and to brief him about Akim and Bangistan. He personally knew little if anything about the country and set several agents on the case to come up with a report in double quick time. O'Reilly's biggest surprise was to discover that the United States had not only an Embassy but an Ambassador, a certain Winkelmeier, in Petrobangorski. The President, of course, knew even less about Bangistan than O'Reilly and certainly didn't remember appointing anybody to represent America's interests there.

After hearing some basic facts about the country and its regime and listening to a summary of the current situation, Rump flicked through the sheaf of papers on which the CIA had printed all of Akim's tweets to date. He looked up at the Director, who had not been invited to take a seat and stood nervously in front of the Oval Office bureau, and said: "I'll take care of this." It was precisely what O'Reilly had feared. He knew what it meant.

An hour later, the President fired the first broadside out of the White House. The tweet read: "Akim, buddy, you don't know who you're dealing with. Maybe it escaped your tiny mind, but I have 1,000 nuclear missiles pointed at you RIGHT NOW. Think about it, loser, before you open your big mouth again."

"Me too," the comment on his post came back fifteen minutes later. "My nuclear missiles pointed at you also, many targets, Coney Island, Yankee Stadium, Madison Square Garden. Think about THAT, loser."

Rump called O'Reilly, who had gone back to his office.

"You didn't mention they had nukes, O'Reilly – long-range ones too."

"They don't," O'Reilly reassured him. "Akim's just bluffing. We've seen no activity at all in that area in three decades."

Rump switched his telephone back to Twitter and shot back to Akim: "HAHA. No you don't! That's bullshit and you know it. So, go screw a goat. One more threat and you're TOAST!"

Three days later, the headlines of the world's media announced in a thousand languages: "Bangistan Fires Intercontinental Test Missile. Lands in Caspian Sea. Leader Hakim Akim Promises – 'New York Harbor Next Time'."

CHAPTER 8

AIMING FOR THE MORAL HIGH GROUND

The Americans reacted swiftly to the Bangistan threat. Within hours, they decided to do nothing.

In the meantime, Rump ordered Zebriski, O'Reilly and Holden to confer and to get back to him with a response strategy. The President promised solemnly that he would refrain from sending any new tweets to Akim until they had done so.

For once, the three men were in total agreement about the way forward. The hour had come for diplomacy. And that was Holden's province. His colleagues invited him to take the lead and to come back to them as soon as possible with his ideas. They would then go together to the White House to present them.

No one, not even his closest colleagues, could really figure Holden out. And since he was not given to introspection, that included the Secretary himself. Holden left soul searching to his enemies, those within the nation – the liberals and socialists – or those without, and that included pretty much everybody. Since his own mind, and soul such that it was, were not given to self-analysis, Holden had fully embraced paranoia and loathing as a substitute. Whatever the issue, he was always two or three conspiracies ahead of everyone. The world was out to harm the United States of America and he was going to make damn sure that the US harmed it first.

Unlike Yogi Akim, his Bangistani counterpart, Holden did not strangle and shoot people (though no one knew much about his private life, it was true). But this was probably only a question of circumstances, of what was possible in the environment into which he had been thrust. That kind of thing just didn't go down well in Washington D.C. and he refrained from it.

But perhaps this is my big chance, thought the Secretary of State, as he sat alone in his office mulling over options for a response to Bangistan's aggression. Perhaps God has sent me the Akims to prove a point. Indeed, at that moment Holden actually thought he heard the good Lord's voice, conveying the message that he alone was charged to bring to the world: "Don't fuck with America." Yes, that was it.

It was far too long since the point had been made effectively. The Russians continued to screw them in Syria, as they had done in Ukraine; the Europeans were dallying still with the mullahs in Tehran, when Washington had ordered them, in no uncertain terms, to cut it out; America had failed miserably to whip the Taliban in Afghanistan and, though they would pretend otherwise, would soon come home defeated; Irak was a total, unspeakable shambles, most likely for the rest of time; Libya was still embroiled in violence, long after they had removed Gaddafi from the picture; US support to the Saudis against the Yemeni Houthis was leading nowhere and only getting America a bad name. Sure, the President was yelling about final victory over the so-called Islamic State, but he was convincing nobody. All said, it was not a pretty picture for the stature and reputation of the most powerful country in the world.

America clearly needed to assert itself anew, to become great again, as the President promised, to show its authority and dominance, "to win a war, for Christ's sake," as Holden put it to his entourage regularly. "It's been far too long," he insisted.

Perhaps the Akims were the ideal fall guys, the lambs for Holden's slaughter? If America couldn't prevail over ignorant losers like those bozos, they might as well *all* give up and go and play golf. The stars were perfectly aligned for a real coup, that was sure. The sorry little country had no allies; no one, not the Chinese, nor the Russians, would come to its rescue, defend it or even protest at the United Nations Security Council, except perhaps to piss off Rump. Not only would America be thanked and fêted for ending a regime of terror, for freeing the Bangistani people from enslavement (with a little collateral damage, it was true), it would again be feared, which in Holden's eyes was by far the most important of desired outcomes.

The only problem he could see was Bangistan's newly-revealed nuclear weapons capability and intercontinental ballistic programme. That's not something to mess with, thought Holden. But maybe their missiles couldn't reach America after all? Maybe they would only knock out London in the first strike, before a rain of American missiles hit them? No one would care too much about that. It might even take a weight off Europe's shoulders.

But his colleagues were right. Proper procedures must be seen to be respected and a diplomatic solution to the crisis must be the first endeavor, even though those fools in Petrobangorski had clearly identified themselves from the start as the belligerent force, as the aggressors, which would permit America to claim any and all of its actions as legitimate self-defence.

"I think the President should meet Akim," Holden told O'Reilly and Zebriski when they came over to the State Department a little later.

"Go on," they invited him in unison.

"Frankly, we've got nothing to lose and everything to gain. It's vital in diplomacy to get the upper hand morally before you start killing people," said Holden.

"Not to put too fine a point on it," said Zebriski.

Holden ignored the Defense Secretary's jab and continued his argument.

"Bangistan is the aggressor, that's already established. Their multiple insults, specific threats, and now this missile test, close the case on that before anyone can even open it. But decorum demands that we make one bid, at least, for peace before taking military action. If the President announces that he's willing to discuss all this, man to man, face to face, with Akim, to seek an end to the conflict together, we are absolutely in the clear to do whatever we like. Are you with me?"

O'Reilly and Zebriski did not hesitate long. The plan might avert a war and, if it didn't, it at least gave them time to position themselves as the seekers of peace.

The three men quickly came to agreement. Holden would contact Winkelmeier, their newly-discovered man in Petrobangorski, and get him to pitch a Rump-Akim summit meeting immediately. They were all sure that Akim would jump at the chance to meet the US President; they knew also that Rump would seize this opportunity to display his legendary art of deal-making and shine once more.

Each of the men carried out of the discussion and its conclusions a different ambition.

Zebriski, a decorated veteran, epitomized the modern armed forces commander. He was the last man who wanted war, either conventional or, God forbid, nuclear. He had seen the horror of the battlefield, of lives destroyed indiscriminately, of the broken bodies of children lying in the ruins of their homes; he had seen his comrades fall in their thousands. He ardently hoped that a settlement could be found with Bangistan without a shot or a missile being fired. Rump was perhaps not the best man to achieve this result, but he was the only man they had.

O'Reilly didn't like the idea of war either. Once the canons roared, intelligence became more or less superfluous to requirements and his undercover agents were shoved aside by uniformed louts who, far from concealing their identity and rank, displayed it with fancy embroidery all over their chests and caps. Sometimes he thought he hated his nation's military leaders a lot more than his intelligence counterparts in hostile countries. He was still nostalgic about the early years of his CIA career, when the Soviet Union had been his playground. He boasted that he had once had a vodka or two with Vladimir Putin in Dresden, where the Russian leader, going under the alias 'Adamov', headed the unlikely Soviet-German House of Friendship. Intelligence operatives understood each other perfectly and they had spent a rather unusual hour together exchanging evasive niceties in their peculiar espionage Esperanto, each aware of the other's identity, but speaking nothing of it. For O'Reilly, peace with Bangistan would set a real challenge to his agency and his men. War, on the other hand, would put them completely out of business in that part of the world. Could Rump pull it off, achieve peace? It really was anyone's guess.

Unlike his colleagues, Secretary Holden *knew* that Rump couldn't pull it off, could never strike a meaningful deal with Akim, even if they spent the rest of their lives together, let alone in a one or two day meeting. It was not that the President was incapable of negotiating a deal. As far as Holden was concerned, he was as good as the next man at that. The truth was elsewhere. There was simply no deal to be had. Anyone who thought that Bangistan would give up its nuclear programme without demanding that America do likewise, however insane such a quid pro quo might sound, was living in cloud cuckoo land. Unlike his colleagues, Holden *understood* dictators. He often thought that he could have made a very good one himself if given half a chance. Why on earth would Bangistan renounce the only leverage it had over anybody or anything? Once its nukes were disabled, it would be an easy prey for any unfriendly force to take over. This must be as glaringly obvious to the Akims as it was to him. Total surrender or war would be the only options for Bangistan once the US got through all this obligatory pussy-footing. Holden was sure of it and very happy to be so. Though eager for war, he could at a stretch live with either option. A nice little puppet regime sitting between Russia and China had its attractions too, would be almost as good as an armed conflict. Moscow and Beijing wouldn't like it, of course, wouldn't like it at all. But that was just tough. America was coming back.

As soon as O'Reilly and Zebriski were out of the room, Holden sent an encrypted cable to Winkelmeier: "Offer Akim head-to-head meeting with Rump. Come here personally with answer."

The Ambassador rushed to the Presidential Palace upon receipt of the message, quickly recorded Akim's insane conditions and assent for a summit and his assurance that in the meantime there would be no missiles nor tests, and two hours later managed to get the last flight out to Almaty that evening. Twenty-four hours later, he was in the Oval Office relaying his conversation. It was at this meeting that Rump, as already recounted, had decided to go to Petrobangorski.

CHAPTER 9

THE SECRET IS REVEALED

Hakim Akim was exceedingly pleased with his missile test and took to Twitter to brag about it.

In contrast, Yogi Hakim inexplicably sensed that no good would come of it, for him at least. His intuition was right; it would soon result in his disgrace and banishment from the Palace and a lot of shooting.

As Minister of Defence, another of his nine portfolios in key areas of the Bangistan state apparatus, Yogi Akim had been responsible for making the test's practical arrangements. It was much simpler than he could ever have imagined. He had called the launch site to establish the feasibility and preparation time for a sudden strike and, much to his surprise, learned from his most loyal comrade and friend Bogdanov, who was in charge of operations, that they were in a state of instant readiness, as they had been for thirty-five years under two regimes.

"What else do we have to do here?" Bogdanov explained lugubriously when Akim expressed his astonishment. "We have nothing but this to spend our time on, after all."

Dmitry Ilyich Bogdanov, despite his mournful manner of expressing himself, was an extremely happy man; if you believe, that is, that there is happiness to be found in asceticism. He lived in a cave in the foothills of the Kalimari Mountains, as did his unit of soldiers and engineers and the scientists responsible for Bangistan's nuclear weapons and missile programme. To say that their life there was spartan would be to put too much of a shine on it.

Bogdanov had been left behind when the Soviet Union collapsed and Russia pulled out the troops who had been standing guard for twenty years over its huge stockpile of nuclear warheads and the missiles required to propel them. More precisely, he had hidden himself behind some rocks as the troops clambered aboard the aircraft sent to evacuate them. At the very last moment, he had suddenly had an illumination: This is where I belong; it is this place to which I have been destined and will die, this wild and barren land far from home. Since childhood he had suffered from a religious bent and often dreamt of becoming a monk or a hermit, of turning his back on so-called civilization, of fleeing the company of men. Now he had his chance to do so and took it. Watching the troop carriers disappear into the sun's glare, Bogdanov experienced an ineffable moment of profound peace.

The Russian's new life alone in the desert, feeding off the great piles of tinned rations left behind by the soldiers, praying and meditating, fetching his water from a nearby well, had lasted only three months. Then one day at dawn a small group of Bangistani officials had arrived unannounced on a countrywide mission to verify what the Russian Army had left behind them. Bogdanov had shown them the immense warehouses of deadly weaponry dug deep into the hillsides, together with the three mobile launch pads waiting to roll out of their cathedral-like rock hangars. The men had made a lot of lists and taken countless photographs, had written report after report, and had left.

Not long after, a small airplane flew in, piloted by a teenager who introduced himself as the younger son of the Great Leader Hassan Akim. In other words, Yogi Akim. They had become firm friends right away. Akim saw clearly that Bogdanov was a man without ambition or worldly needs and therefore some one he could trust. Bogdanov saw in

Akim a youth of great greed and hunger for power and pleasure who would leave him alone if he was discrete and obedient. A perfect match for the business that the future Minister of Defence had in mind: making himself rich one day. They parted on good terms and a lot of innuendo about the flourishing market for missiles and warheads that was likely to develop in the disordered post-Soviet world. Akim promised that Bogdanov's terrible solitude would rapidly come to an end and that he would adore his new comrades. Bogdanov hoped and prayed to God that Akim would soon be distracted by other business opportunities and that he and his site would be quickly forgotten.

Bogdanov's supplications to the heavens fell on deaf ears. Soon, three rattling and shaking Antonov military transport aircraft shuddered to a noisy halt on the Kalimari dirt track runway. They spilled out two companies of Bangistani soldiers accompanied by a team of engineers and arms specialists. The major in charge bore a proclamation signed by the Great Leader himself making Bogdanov their Commander. He also received orders to get the base fighting fit and to remain operational.

There had been no discussion after Hassan Akim's untimely and, according to foreign intelligence agencies, *perhaps suspicious* 1995 death, about whether Hakim or Yogi should succeed him, no Shakespearean struggle for power. The elder brother, as was custom in the family and in the country, would assume the throne. Since family and country were the same thing in the case of Bangistan, Hakim became Great Leader in turn. Partly out of a keen political sense, partly out of fear of his ruthless younger brother, he gave Yogi countless titles and responsibilities and a free hand to continue ransacking the nation as their father had done before them. He could personally keep fifty percent of all the money that he could make or find.

Yogi Akim took his new freedom and duties seriously, and immediately set about scouring the length and breadth of the country for fresh sources of wealth. One day, he suddenly remembered Bogdanov and the cavemen of the Kalimari. No news had come in or out of the complex in the three years since the departure of the Russians and their replacement by Bangistani personnel.

Akim renewed communications with his friend, paid him another visit, and there and then in Bogdanov's cave cooked up a wonderful scheme to profit from the useless arsenal hidden there in the mountains – they would sell off a few of the nuclear warheads and missiles to neighboring regimes and various groups of professedly religious bandits who all seemed hell bent on increasing their military strengths.

Contacts were rapidly made, through a string of the shady intermediaries who ply the international arms trade, with the men who had the money. And soon enough, Akim and a compliant Bogdanov found themselves at the heart of a blossoming trade. As Akim had suspected, Bogdanov wanted nothing from the deals, just to be left alone and at peace, as far as this was possible, in his desert.

The Akim vault in the Bahnhofstrasse had twice to be enlarged to accommodate the results of the booming bomb business over the next decade.

All these years later, following the first successful missile test in this new era of a more assertive and belligerent Bangistan, Yogi suggested to Hakim that the Commander of the nuclear base should finally be given a medal and a promotion. The happy President readily agreed and rifled through the motley collection of brass and ribbons in his desk. He gave the prettiest one he could find to Yogi, one on which he hadn't spilt vodka during one of the parties in the Palace at which he displayed a vast array of them on his chest.

"What's it called?" asked Yogi.

"Anything you like," said Hakim. "I think it came from father."

Yogi christened it there and then as "Knight First Class in the Order of the White Rose of Bangistan" and vowed to pin it on Bogdanov personally.

As he left his brother's office, Hakim called after him to warn Commander Bogdanov to prepare for a second test for the following week. This time he wanted the missile to go further, to the Black Sea.

"Isn't that a bit too close to Europe?" asked Yogi.

"Indeed," said the President, beaming with pleasure. "That's the whole idea."

That afternoon, Yogi Akim flew his private jet to the Kalimari Mountains for the last time.

"I have a wonderful surprise for you," he announced to Bogdanov, who greeted him on the dirt track runway. "You are now a Knight! Courtesy of the Great Leader himself."

"Thanks. I shall wear it at the Kalimari Cocktail Club," said Bogdanov drily, as he took the grubby ribbon and medal from Akim's hands.

Yes, Bogdanov was an ascetic, who had willingly given up the pleasures of life to live and work in this godforsaken hole in which, paradoxically, he found himself closer to God than he had been at any other time of his life. Only one vice had escaped the otherwise abstemious rituals of his existence. He couldn't resist a glass or two of vodka from time to time, either on the pretext of the few celebrations that came his way or in his brief moments of depression. But what more appropriate occasion could there be than his elevation to knighthood to break open a new bottle? Even his conscience couldn't find an argument against *that*. He and Akim thus headed to his grim cave for a toast or two.

"We are so very pleased with the test, you can't imagine,"

Akim told Bogdanov after a few glasses. "So much so that we are going to ask you for another one! Next week some time. But we shall send the missile even further this time – into the Black Sea. You can do it, of course?"

"The Black Sea? I was born and spent my infant years in Novorossiysk, you know. Very fond memories. Let's drink to our childhoods, Yogi!"

He poured them another glass, they entwined arms, and both declared loudly, "To childhood!"

"And the test next week?" Akim enquired.

"Impossible, alas," said Bogdanov.

"Technically? I thought you told me that we could even reach America if we wanted to."

"No, the distance isn't a problem at all, we Russians saw to that many, many years ago. But we don't have any missiles left. The Caspian was the very last one."

"What are you talking about, no missiles? Are you drunk, Dmitry? These hills are full of missiles and nuclear warheads, have you forgotten?"

"They were, they were indeed," said Bogdanov nostalgically. "Not a single one left of either, though."

They were clean out of bombs.

This was the most secret of Bangistan's many secrets.

Seeing the distressed, paralysed look on Akim's face, Bogdanov patiently and rather drunkenly explained how the entire arsenal had been sold off to the traffickers, and detailed all the orders he had fulfilled at Akim's command. Truck after truck had come and shipped them out after Akim had received payment and given his assent. He had all the details, all the paperwork, if Yogi would like to see it. Everything was accounted for.

"What about the test last week, then?" asked Akim desperately.

"There, Yogi, I have a confession to make. I cannot lie. I

cheated those dirty Iranians on their last shipment."

Bogdanov had held one missile back, for sentimental reasons, and now even this was at the bottom of the Caspian Sea.

Akim said nothing. After a few minutes staring coldly into Bogdanov's eyes, he got up, went over to the telecommunications cave, ordered everyone out, and made a telephone call. They did not speak further that day or that night.

Akim and Bogdanov awoke just after dawn to the sound of helicopters and machine gun fire. Looking out from Bogdanov's cave entrance, they saw soldiers leaping to the ground and dashing, firing wildly, into all the other caves on the hillside. The carnage lasted no more than ten minutes. None of the base soldiers or other employees armed themselves at night and had no defence; the killing was easy. The captain of the helicopter troop soon rushed up to them, saluted Akim, and announced his job complete. Akim instructed him to fly back to Petrobangorski and to keep his mouth shut until he heard from him again.

Only two living men were left in the foothills of the Kalimari Mountains. After a while, one of them broke the silence.

"I have to shoot you too, my old friend, you know that, don't you?" Akim told Bogdanov.

The Russian smiled and said, softly, "I know." He fell to his knees, still smiling, and clasped his hands in prayer. Bogdanov had never been so happy in his life as at this moment of his death.

Akim went behind the kneeling man, took out both his Luger pistols, and fired a bullet from each of them into the back of Bogdanov's head.

Up until this moment, Akim had never seen any profit in religious belief, but now made a mental note to reconsider the question. "If a man can die with such a smile on his face …" he said to himself. "What if?"

Akim forgot this brief Pascalian moment even before he reached his airplane at the end of the dirt runway. He had more important things to think about than God – how to announce this terrible, tragic news to his brother, for instance.

It took Yogi Akim three days to summon up the courage to visit the Presidential Palace again. In the meantime, he had work to do, most notably the elimination of the entire helicopter combat squadron who had wiped out the missile programme unit at Kalimari.

Once in front of his Great Leader brother, and in response to Hakim Akim's first question – "Is the new test all arranged?" – he had come out with it: "We have no more missiles and not even a single warhead."

This information so stunned the President that he could not find a word to say, though saliva began to form at the edges of his mouth.

Yogi leapt into the breach and blurted out the whole story about the loyal Bogdanov's 'betrayal', leaving out a few details about his own inattention to the dwindling and, finally, total depletion of the weapons stock.

He informed the President that everyone had been shot on the site, including the recently knighted Bogdanov. The troops he had called in to shoot them had, in turn, all now been shot too. Their executions had taken place that very morning.

"They died shouting 'Long life to President Akim', 'Forgive us Great Leader' and 'We failed you'." Yogi was actually telling the truth, though he really didn't understand how people could spout such rubbish while they were facing their benefactor's firing squad.

After a few more minutes, the President finally spoke. "What about the execution squad? You shot them too, of course?"

"No," replied Yogi. "We had to shoot the soldiers who

shot the personnel of the missile unit, because they were aware of the secret. But the men who shot *them* didn't know anything; they had no idea why they were killing them, not a clue." He had thus spared them; otherwise there would logically be no end to the shooting and he had other things to do.

"I should certainly shoot *you*, though," said Hakim thoughtfully. He had regained his composure with incredible rapidity and, as the strategist that he was known to be, was already looking ahead. "There's no doubt about that at all, you blundering idiot."

"Mother wouldn't like it if you did that," said Yogi sheepishly.

"I'll have her shot too!" shouted Hakim.

Yogi Akim laughed at this jest and left the President to his anger. He would never again be allowed to set foot in the Presidential Palace ...

In the meantime, he had an appointment with Winkelmeier to visit a labour camp together. It was a nice day for such a trip.

Left alone, Hakim Akim let loose a string of terrible obscenities into the empty room.

Yogi had always been useful to Hakim. One could not run a dictatorship without eliminating people, and his brother was very good at this. It was indeed the great good fortune of the Akim dynasty that its latest scions were such *complementary* psychopaths. Hakim was far too squeamish, perhaps too sentimental even, to watch an execution, let alone to kill anyone himself. This was why he was happy to have a brother who enjoyed both these activities. In their shared childhood – only sixteen months separated their births – Hakim had even been obliged to turn his head away when Yogi cut off the front legs of lizards to see if they could still manage to walk.

Hakim had in common with the majority of ordinary people everywhere that if killing and other atrocities take place out of their sight and don't touch anyone they care about personally, they don't really think that much about it, if indeed at all. It doesn't move them.

Hakim Akim, of course, actually *ordered* incarceration, torture, starvation and murder, but once the paperwork had been done, he thought no further of the victims, didn't dwell upon their fate.

As for the ordinary people, one might think that only those who live in terror in dictatorships like Bangistan deserve our absolution for choosing to ignore it.

CHAPTER 10

QUASIMODO AT LA ROTONDE

"So, Akim 'loved the DVDs'," said Blakely with a theatrical wink as he sat down.

"Yes. We don't know what the hell that meant either."

"Come on," Blakely insisted.

"No, really. It was *jolly good* of us to share the report in the first place," said Schurz. "You don't think we'd then take the trouble to hide anything from you, do you *old chap*?"

Blakely laughed. "You can cut out the silly English accent, Scott. No, I suppose not, but it's an odd thing to put in a cable if even *you* don't understand it. Do you know this man Winkelmeier personally?"

"Not at all. That's another odd thing. No one at all knew him or knew he was sitting there in Petrobangorski until this whole Bangistan thing blew up – to coin a phrase. The forgotten Stan had a forgotten US Ambassador."

"Sounds like it's a good place to get away from it all," said Blakely. "Or was, in any case."

Stephen Blakely and Scott Schurz, counterparts in the British and US embassies, were at La Rotonde, their favorite brasserie, in Montparnasse. It was there that they met once a month to eat, drink and share jokes and, from time to time, to exchange information that might justify their expense accounts. That evening, they had a lot to talk about, as Blakely had to file a report – "directly to London," he underlined - suggesting how the Prime Minister might handle the Bangistan question in the Versailles talks.

"In what mood, in what frame of mind, is Rump coming

to the meetings?" asked Blakely.

"The President is very excited indeed about the G7 agenda," said Schurz soberly.

"Really? That's good to hear."

"Sure. Gender equality, climate change, the fight against poverty, actions for peace, education … Rump is passionate about all these issues."

Blakely nodded with satisfaction.

Schurz wiped the filet's *sauce au poivre* from his lips with a serviette, took a gulp of his wine, looked earnestly at his British friend, and burst into uncontrollable, raucous laughter that could be heard all over the restaurant.

Loud Americans were no more popular in La Rotonde and among its discrete and elite clientele than anywhere else in Paris. But there was something quite magical, completely infectious, in Schurz's hilarity that no one at all could ever resist. When an embarrassed Blakely, British to the core, looked around in shame, expecting to encounter a wall of reproving glares, he saw only broad smiles and heard nothing but tittering from every table.

"You English have too much good faith," the American continued. "The State Department thinks that the French cooked up that agenda as revenge for Rump's behavior in Quebec last year. *C'est une provocation, mon ami*! No, our beloved President doesn't give a shit for all that, of course. But Bangistan, that's another pair of sleeves, *une autre paire de manches*, as the French have it. There, he's all wound up and ready to go for gold. The Peacemaker-in-Chief himself. He's already reserved his place in history, in fact."

"And do you have ideas yet what it is that he'll propose to Akim?"

"The problem, *mon ami*, if I can be totally blunt with you, is that it doesn't matter in the slightest what is discussed, advised and decided in advance, in Washington or in Versailles.

Rump will play it totally by ear, wing it anyhow, and will have forgotten, deliberately or otherwise, all our counsel and strategy proposals even before he gets off the plane in Petrobangorski."

"That's rather terrifying, isn't it?" remarked Blakely.

"That's what we have to deal with, anyway; we're getting used to it. But in answer to your question, the desired scenario is this: President Rump will demand that Bangistan instantly give up its nuclear tests, destroy all its warheads, and abandon its intercontinental missile programme."

"And in exchange?"

"Money, lots and lots of it for many years to come. And there, we are going to ask you good folks to chip in, too, and pay your share for world peace. But we don't have to talk about that just yet."

"It all seems improbable to me, Scott. What makes Rump or anyone else think that Akim will go for it?"

"Well, it's not very original, but the President is unshakably convinced that every man has his price, as the saying goes. He doesn't see why Hakim Akim should be any different. And we certainly know from Winkelmeier that the Akim family loves money more than anything else at all. Why otherwise would they have lived all these years in isolation, almost in secrecy, without caring at all to make their mark on the international scene. Amassing a fortune has been their only goal. And we know very well that men who love money love nothing more than getting more of it, however wealthy they are. They simply can't stop, nothing is ever enough. It's practically a disease but, after all, it's also the foundation of our precious capitalistic system, so we can't complain too much."

"And if the adage is wrong and Akim won't take the money, what then?"

"Bye, bye Bangistan, I guess. Here today, gone tomorrow.

America at your service."

They enjoyed their dinner, laughed a lot, and between them drank three excellent bottles of wine to world peace. Before they got up to leave, Schurz proposed one last joke that he had picked up that week.

"Go ahead," smiled Blakely.

Most people who laugh at their own jokes before or while they are telling them kill in the bud all possible desire of the others to find them funny. Schurz, however, was a unique case. He was a grand master, an artist of the joke, who flooded his stories with the light and joy of so much of his own laughter that this became a spectacle of amusement in itself.

"Great!" began Schurz enthusiastically with a bellow of laughter to set the mood. "Quasimodo was in his bell tower in Notre Dame waiting to see if his classified ad in Le Figaro that day would bring any candidates for the bell-ringing job that had just been vacated. Soon, he heard a knock on the belfry door and in walked this middle-aged dwarf. Not only was the poor chap's growth stunted, he had no arms! 'I 'av come for the job!' said the dwarf. 'But you 'av no arms,' protested Quasimodo. 'No problem, I show you,' said the dwarf, who stepped under the giant bell, pressed his nose against its inner edge, and began to walk forwards, then backwards, forwards then backwards, taking the bell with him as he moved and it began to ring.

"At one point he stopped, looked out at Quasimodo, pointed to his large nose, and said proudly: 'You see! I can do it!' At this moment, however, the bell swung back, hit the dwarf in the head, and sent him hurtling out of the cathedral window and two hundred feet down onto the stone fore-court. Quasimodo rushed down the three hundred or so steps and out of the church, where he saw a bloodied, crushed corpse surrounded by gendarmes. One of them asked him: 'Monsieur Quasimodo, do you know zis man?' 'No, I'm afraid not,' said the hunchback, shaking his head. 'But his face *does* ring a bell'."

At this point Schurz howled with convulsive laughter and Blakely too. "Stop, *arrête*," cried Schurz, "It ees not fineeshed, my story." He went on:

"Two hours later, having made a police statement and returned to his belfry, Quasimodo hears another knock on the door. Unbelievably, another dwarf walks in, he too without arms. They were identical, could have been twins! This guy gives the same spiel and offers a demonstration of how he can ring the giant bell with his head. And so he does. But again, full of pride at his prowess, he makes the same mistake as the first candidate. He stops, turns to Quasimodo to speak, and bang-a-boom, smack in his back the bell hits him, propelling him in turn out of the tower and down upon the screaming crowds below. Once more, the hunchback makes the long run down to the cathedral entrance and finds the same gendarmes examining the body. The same policeman as before, sighing, asks him: 'And so, Quasimodo, what about *zis* man? Do you know him?' 'No, *je regrette, Monsieur le gendarme*, I do not know him either. But what I *can* say, is that he is a dead ringer for the first guy.'"

While Blakely giggled compulsively, Schurz slapped his knees and punched the air with glee as if it was the first time he had ever heard the joke too.

When their mirth had faded, Blakely reached into the pocket of his jacket and pulled out a photograph. "One last thing, Scott, on the subject of dead ringers, I almost forgot. Take a look at this."

Schurz held the picture and shrugged. "So, one more shot of my Great Leader?"

"His real or imagined dissimulations include being a transvestite, then? Look closer, he's wearing a dress." It was true that this wasn't clear at first, since the photograph was cut short just below the waist.

"So he is, how odd. The Russians? MI6? Who's putting this around, Stephen?"

"Nobody, Scott, Ruth – she sends her best regards by the way – took it while we were on holiday last week. This isn't Rump at all. I'm so glad you fell for it. We were amazed too."

"Who is it then? It's an unbelievable resemblance."

"She's called Marie-Pierre and she sells zucchini in a village near the Pyrenees."

"I've rarely seen such identical people," said Schurz. "Can I keep the photograph?"

"By all means. I brought it with that in mind."

At that, they broke up the dinner and each went home, promising to call one another at the slightest Bangistan news. Two weeks later, they would in any case meet again, when their little club of G7 diplomats had their three-monthly shindig.

CHAPTER 11

WINKELMEIER VISITS
A MODEL CAMP

It took a lot of courage for Ambassador Winkelmeier to visit the camp, but the State Department had insisted on it. It was a key step in Holden's strategy to storm and capture the moral high ground before inviting the military to open fire and finish off the job.

Yogi Akim was not at all his usual grinning self as he picked Winkelmeier up on the road in front of the Embassy in his Lincoln.

"Just push those aside," he said, pointing to a bazooka and a brace of machine guns lying on the back seat as Winkelmeier climbed into the car.

Akim muttered an order to the driver beside him and they set off, accompanied by a handful of his personal guards riding Harley-Davidsons in front and behind them.

Winkelmeier was surprised to see the bikes and asked Akim how they had come to buy them.

"They were part of another deal you don't want to know about, Ambassador. Let's leave it at that."

They rode on silently through the ugly, interminable gas fields that blighted the landscape around Petrobangorski, a thousand steel towers and miles of pipeline glinting in the sunlight. A lot had happened in the past few days and they were both still thinking it through. Winkelmeier couldn't sleep at night contemplating the forthcoming Rump trip and all the possibilities it held for being a comprehensive disaster.

Akim, oppressed with the weight of his dreadful secret about the vanished arms stock, believed at that moment that he was the loneliest man in the world. He so wished that Olga would agree to come to Bangistan and give him the whipping he so thoroughly deserved, since Hakim had forbidden him to leave the country again for the time being.

Just to change his thoughts and strike up conversation, Winkelmeier leaned forward and asked Akim's back: "How is it that you speak such excellent English and your brother not a word of it? I've been meaning to ask you for a long time."

"Hakim was more clever as a child than I, Winkelmeier," said Akim without turning round. "He divined the future. Our father lived in awe of you Americans, your military power, your movie stars, your wealth, your great sportsmen – I got my name from Yogi Berra, as you know – and urged us both to learn your tongue. Hakim refused, saying that the USA was a country of the past, and that the future lay in the hands of China. My father told him that the Chinese were just a bunch of ignorant, filthy peasants and would remain that way for centuries, but Hakim only laughed. Within a few years he was speaking fluent Mandarin and striking up relations with Chinese officials. And he was right, Winkelmeier, of course, now we see the decline of your country and the incredible rise in strength of our excellent neighbors."

Winkelmeier smiled. "Let's judge on the long haul, Akim. We're not finished yet and many interesting things will happen in China, you know, in the years ahead."

"Such as?"

"The real problems will begin when economic growth can no longer be sustained at its current high levels and tens, perhaps hundreds of millions of people slump back into relative poverty. Who will they hold responsible? The Communist

Party, of course. Why do you think Xi has been arresting more and more people in recent years, clamping down on every hint of opposition to his policies, eliminating anyone who challenges the political status quo? What magic secret do you think the Party holds that will prevent the Chinese from going the same way as the Soviets?"

"They are less stupid and not half as lazy as the Russians – and they don't read Pushkin," said Akim.

"*Pushkin*?"

"Or Dostoevsky, or Tolstoy, that whole gang of rebels, anarchists and revolutionaries. Those literature-loving Russians could never burn Pushkin, that glorificator of '*liberty*'. They banned and murdered countless new authors and left those 19th century criminals on the shelves of every home in the country!"

"Interesting theory," said Winkelmeier. "I'm sure that your own, Bangistani writers must appreciate the importance and influence you give to literature."

"What Bangistani writers?" asked Akim. "We are not fools like the Russians. Writing is not allowed here. We don't waste our time deciding what's bad, what's harmless, what's dangerous. No, you will not see many books in this country, my friend. Except a few on the thoughts of the Great Leader, of course, which, between you and me, he did not write personally.

"Do you know that my father once tried to get that South American poet – what was his name? – Oh, yes, Pablo Neruda, to write him a beautiful little ode, as he did for Stalin? Even with a very handsome price offer, he declined. He must have run out of inspiration." And at this, Akim broke into verse.

" 'To be men! That is the Stalinist law! ... We must learn from Stalin, his sincere intensity, his concrete clarity ... Stalin is the noon, the maturity of man and of peoples. Stalinists, let us bear this title with pride ... Et cetera, et cetera' ... Very beautiful, don't you think, this Neruda, Winkelmeier?"

"We differ in our view of Stalin, I'm afraid," said Winkelmeier, leaving it at that.

Warming to the subject, Akim went on: "The Chinese are not taking any chances in this respect. They ban or censor everything they don't like, from the past, the present and the future. They repress practically everyone who has any opinion at all and that necessarily includes writers – artists too, of course. They learnt the lessons of the Soviet collapse, just like us. Do not give an inch, not the breadth of a goat's hair, to the enemies of the interior!"

"I still think that in time China will collapse," Winkelmeier persisted. "I don't know if it will happen in our lifetimes, to tell the truth, but it's all going to end one day in revolt and bloodshed, you can be sure of it."

"Maybe it will be so also in America?" ventured Akim. "Another civil war, perhaps, from what I hear?" He laughed.

After an hour on the road, they pulled up to the entrance of Camp 77. The iron gates were quickly thrown wide and they drove a few yards more before stopping between two long lines of inmates. Guards opened the limousine doors and as Akim and Winkelmeier stepped out, the prisoners began to sing, in English, with the appropriate gestures:

"If you're happy and you know it, clap your hands! If you're happy and you know it, clap your hands! If you're happy and you know it, then your face will surely show it, clap your hands."

Winkelmeier thought that he had never seen such hatred and despair on any faces in his life. And they were looking at *him*, trying to catch *his* eyes. He was particularly distressed to see that there were children among the prisoners, though their eyes seemed blank and expressed nothing at all.

"Welcome to a typical Bangistani education camp!" said

Akim. "This is not one of the nicest, but it will give you an idea of how kindly we deal with our criminals, Winkelmeier. We don't know why your government insisted so much on this visit, but I can tell you right now that the Great Leader is going to ask Rump to arrange such a tour for us also. Rikers Island, perhaps. Or Guantanamo Bay," he added with a wink.

"Those aren't concentration camps, Akim, they're prisons."

"I don't personally see much of a difference," said Akim. "We hold criminals, both of us, let's not split the hair of the goat, shall we?"

There's all the difference in the world, thought the Ambassador, but I know it's completely futile to have a debate with Akim about it, now or probably at any time. He simply ventured: "You know very well the difference, Akim. These are *political* prisoners, people detained for their *opinions*, not common criminals; for those you have other jails. I hear that you visit them often, actually."

Akim ignored this last remark, though he did wonder where Winkelmeier got his information.

"We all have our different definitions of criminal, Ambassador. Here in Bangistan, it is a crime to dissent and oppose the state in word or deed. You must understand that."

"Anyhow, let's get on with the visit, for my report, and get out of here," urged Winkelmeier. "In the meantime, perhaps you'd also explain what on earth the children are doing here. What were their 'crimes'?"

"We believe in the family, Winkelmeier, very strongly. We do not want to break them up because of one black sheep. So we bring in everybody, young and old. I think it is most merciful of us."

"You are really shameless, Akim," Winkelmeier let out, instantly regretting his undiplomatic words and reminding himself that his duties did not include berating the representatives of host nations.

But Akim didn't seem to mind. As they walked in between the first wooden barracks, which stretched out as far as the eye could see, both in front and at their sides, he responded casually: "That's quite true, Mr. Ambassador. I was never taught shame and I've never seen any profit at all in acquiring it. It is by far the most useless of emotions, don't you think? Shame is a vice that only the innocent can afford."

"So, you admit that you are not innocent?" asked Winkelmeier.

"Of course. You may take me to be a brute, Ambassador, but please don't think that I'm a fool."

"'Shame is a vice that only the innocent can afford'," Winkelmeier repeated to himself. He couldn't decide whether this was a profound insight or absolute rubbish.

"Come on, Winkelmeier, don't destroy our nice little trip with, what do you call them, *insinuations*," Akim said cheerfully, taking his hand and leading him further on up the main alley of the camp, pointing out a football field and a basketball court on the way.

They briefly visited one of the long huts, where three-level bunk beds lined all the walls and the center of the room, which was deserted.

"Where are all the people?" asked Winkelmeier.

"Oh, they are out in the fields, working and singing," said Akim.

"How long has this concentration camp been here?"

"Why do you insist on this term *concentration*, Winkelmeier? It has nasty overtones in your mouth, I think."

"Yes, it does, indeed."

"Well, after all, you can call it what you want, my friend. What do I care? Detention camp, labor camp, education camp, relocation camp, reform camp, concentration camp.

Holiday camp!" he laughed.

"That's not amusing, Akim, not at all. But how did this camp come to be built?"

"That is an interesting story, Winkelmeier, I'm glad that you ask. Well, in the good old days, the Soviets took care of all our problematic people by kindly making place for them in their gulag, a system which existed under one name or another up until the collapse of the empire and, say cynics, still exists today, more or less.

"When the Russians left Bangistan, I was still a very young man and my father thought it would be an excellent educational project for me to research and write a proposal for him on the creation of a new penal apparatus to take care of our own people. I studied detention camps of many kinds. You might be surprised by what I found."

"Tell me," said Winkelmeier.

"Many would argue that it was you Americans, in fact, who invented the concentration camp – the 'reservations' to which you forcefully dragged Indians two hundred years ago already."

"We call them 'Native Americans', actually."

"But John Wayne didn't, did he?"

"Be that as it may, times have changed, terminology has evolved."

"Very well. So, if we accept that the Indian reservations were the first enforced concentrations of groups of people, ethnic in this case …"

"Which I don't," said Winkelmeier, "it was more complicated than that."

"Surely, surely," smiled Akim. "It's always more complicated to explain when the crimes are your own, Winkelmeier, isn't it?"

The Ambassador replied simply: "Go on."

"The next part is quite funny, actually, even ironical, I

would say. If we accept that your Indian 'reservations' don't count, it was the Spanish who invented the concentration camp, in Cuba. Did you know this? The word actually comes from their language, *reconcentración*. They rounded up all the doubtful civilians, which included everybody, of course, because the Spanish are a most suspicious people, and put them all behind barbed wire, where one hundred and fifty thousand died of the brutal conditions and starvation, which was the general idea ... Anyhow, here comes the ironic part that you will like."

"I doubt it," said Winkelmeier.

"The Americans, particularly the press, were scandalized by these camps, and made martyrs of these people. Even your President – McInley, I think it was – described them as places of 'extermination' of the Cuban peasants. He used that precise word, Winkelmeier. However, when America defeated Spain and took over many of its colonies, it quickly discovered the virtues of having your enemies, the rebels against colonization, gathered together in one spot. You began creating and running concentration camps yourself, all over the place, Cuba, the Philippines ..."

Akim was unstoppable on the subject. He did pause a moment, though, and asked Winkelmeier, "Perhaps I am making you a little uncomfortable, Mr. Ambassador?"

"Go on," Winkelmeier said once more.

"Very well! Next in line are thought to be your friends the British, who created concentration camps in South Africa, where they confined tens of thousands of Boer women and children and let them perish. At that stage, practically everyone was in on the game. The Germans – already! – massacred seventy thousand of the rebel Herrero in camps in Namibia; a whole league of nations went on to create their concentration camps all over the world. They became quite *à la mode*, Winkelmeier. And I haven't yet quite finished with your case, either. You nice Americans, as you know, locked up more than one hundred thousand people of Japanese heritage, most of them your own nationals, during the last world war."

"Wartime is different, Akim, you know that. A nation has to protect itself."

"I do believe Herr Hitler said something similar, Winkelmeier. But we are always at war, aren't we? Here in Bangistan we wage a daily war against our heretics, the dangerous, misguided people who would try and bring us down. This is why we put them out of harm's way here and there, like in this camp. Anyhow, to conclude my history lesson – I have barely mentioned the Nazi and communist cases, Winkelmeier, but then you are very well informed about those already, I would imagine – I would invite you to concede my point: We have invented *nothing*, whatever you want to call these places. So you see, perhaps, after all, *none* of us are innocent?"

"Perhaps, but we are here today in Bangistan and you are speaking of history," Winkelmeier said weakly. "At least we're trying to be better."

"Yet I have seen children in cages in your country just recently, Winkelmeier. This we would never do, you know. You are not so pure as you think, you Americans. You think that because you commit your misdeeds in the name of 'democracy' that you are more moral than the rest of us. One day, probably when the Chinese crush you, you will see that the world does not necessarily agree."

Akim had become quite heated and looked as though he wanted to shoot someone, perhaps an American, right there and then, so Winkelmeier held his peace and wandered off down a side alley. He saw in the distance another compound, behind other fences, where many people milled around. Unlike the other inmates he had encountered, who wore simple, uniform, prison garments, these other people were dressed in a colorful array of civilian clothes, and all the men wore four-cornered, flat, cloth skullcaps. Akim caught him by the shoulder and stopped him from going further. "Who are they?" asked Winkelmeier, pointing down the alley.

"Don't worry your head about that, Ambassador," said Akim. And then, after a pause: "I shouldn't tell you, but I will if you promise me that you won't put it in your report. I know that you are a good, honest man and won't break your word on this."

"Alright, since I won't find out otherwise."

Akim smiled. "They, my friend, are a business diversification." He paused to let Winkelmeier's curiosity sharpen. "They are worth a lot of money to me, so we take extra special care of them. They are not, as you see from their dress, Bangistani. They are Chinese!"

"You are imprisoning *Chinese* people?"

"For an excellent price, my friend. It seems that Beijing has temporarily run out of concentration camps and while they are building some new ones, perhaps, they have outsourced the job to me … to us, I mean. We have more camps than we need and some spare space – we overestimated the number of people who would, what should we say, inexplicably express *doubt* about the Great Leader and his policies. Those people over there are Uighurs, vaguely related to us, so it's said. In that way, they perhaps feel more at home. Haha! They are shipped in from time to time by the governor of their so-called autonomous region, who has been given orders to lock them all up. Yes," he reiterated, "it's a very good sideline."

What a disgrace, thought Winkelmeier. But when a man has no moral sense, not a trace of it, and Yogi Akim was such a man, there is simply no limit to the vileness of the acts he is prepared to commit, no gradation in his depravity. Unless other men can obstruct him, that is, unless there is resistance.

Winkelmeier hadn't discovered anything in this charade, nor had he expected to. He suspected that this 'model' camp was in fact a transit station towards the real things in the north and west of the country. He didn't think any of the people had been here long, judging from the state of their garb and their relative good health. There was only one thing the regime hadn't been able hide from him and that was the desperate look in the prisoners' eyes. They and he both knew only too well what awaited them.

A guard in one of the northern camps had recently escaped across the border into Russia and had found his way to the American embassy in Moscow where he had sought and been granted asylum. Winkelmeier had unearthed his account of the camp on a recent trip to Washington. It spoke of horror defying the imagination of any sane man. Of skeletal cripples in rags, with torn off ears, smashed eyes and crooked noses, the result of constant torture and beatings. Of the rats, snakes, frogs and insects that they ate to keep somehow alive. Of their labor in mines, where they were simply left, trapped to die, when tunnels collapsed, as they did frequently. Of the authority given to the guards to shoot at will any prisoner who failed to follow orders or did not work enough for their taste. Of more than a thousand deaths each year, from starvation, disease or murder. This, multiplied perhaps fifty times in other locations, was the hidden reality of forgotten Bangistan.

And here Winkelmeier found himself on a day out in the sun with one of the chief, unpunished perpetrators of these terrible crimes against humanity. Once the Rump visit was over, he was getting out, resigning, going back to Georgetown and staying there.

Perhaps Holden and his cohort of hawks nesting all over Washington were right: "You can't argue with dictators, Winkelmeier," he had once told him. "The only argument they understand is a bullet in the head."

That night, as he lay in bed in Mrs Winkelmeier's arms, he said to her: "Shame is a vice that only the innocent can afford."

"That's very clever my dear, very true."

"Yes, I was afraid you would say that."

Winkelmeier began to weep, softly at first and then in great fits.

"We're going home, my love, we're going home," he said between sobs.

"Yes, my dear, it's time, I know," his wife replied.

CHAPTER 12

TWO ENGLISHMEN, ONE ROOM, A LEGEND IS BORN

Ormrod's midnight call, on the special line, caught the Ambassador with his pants down. Literally. They were around his ankles, to be precise, as he cavorted in his four-poster embassy bed with a very promising British actress who was looking to break into the French film scene and thought, in the absence of other leads, that this might be the best way to go about it. They had met that evening at the Cinématèque during a celebration of British-French cooperation in film-making, such that it was. Pickering had boasted shamelessly of his glamorous friends in the local movie industry and how he might introduce her to them.

"Give Blakely everything he wants," the Minister ordained. "Anything at all and don't ask why he wants it."

Sir Edmund, who had been cut in his stride, as it were, was grateful that the call was so brief, if a little mysterious, and that Ormrod hung up without further explanation. He hoped that the spell he had cast over the young lady had not been broken …

In the morning, his first instruction to his secretary was to put round a note to all senior staff saying simply: "Give Blakely anything he wants and don't ask why."

Two days later, Blakely found himself on a fast-speed train at the Gare Montparnasse, waiting for a stranger to take the seat opposite him.

"Second class? I'm disappointed," said a man who soon appeared beside him, two cameras hanging round his neck, a tripod under his arm, a bag of lenses in his hand and a rucksack on his back packed with even more equipment.

"What *is* the old country coming to when an important man like you has to travel with the cattle?" he continued while he stuffed the bag and rucksack in the overhead rack.

He introduced himself – "Hawkins" – as he shook Blakely's hand and clambered into his seat. "Pleased to meet you."

"Likewise, I'm sure," said Blakely. "It looks like you brought your whole studio with you."

"You haven't seen half of it. I've got a collapsible umbrella and a video cam up there too. One never knows. You guys are so vague about what it is I have to shoot, that I have to cover all angles. I thought the embassy man mumbled something about 'vegetables' – he was sniggering at the time – but perhaps I misheard. I didn't ask him to clarify; it's not healthy to ask too many questions in this line of work, I've found."

Blakely had indeed mentioned 'vegetables' at the embassy when requesting a photographer, thinking this would be taken as a joke and put everyone off the scent. He had singularly failed in that, it seemed. He must be more careful.

The train soon pulled out of the station and headed south.

"So, the job's in Biarritz then?" enquired Hawkins. "I've been to worse places."

"No, actually. We pick up a hire car there and then drive a few hours."

"That's nice," said Hawkins. "Final destination?"

"You wouldn't have heard of it. You'll see."

Each got out a newspaper, *Le Figaro* for Blakely, *L'Equipe* for Hawkins, and plunged into the political news for the first, and last night's football match reports, for the second. After a while, Blakely looked up and asked, just to make conversation:

"Are you a spy, Hawkins?"

"If I was, I don't think I'd have the liberty to tell you, would I, Sir?"

"We're on the same side, you know."

"Appearances would have that, it's true. But one can be never sure, they say."

"You've been reading too much John Le Carré, Hawkins."

The photographer laughed. "I do like him, it's true. But as for being a spy or not, to be honest I'm not quite sure, Sir."

"Don't call me 'Sir', I'm Stephen. But what do you mean you're not sure?"

"Well, no one ever explains to me why I'm being asked to take pictures of one thing or another. I just answer the call and do what I'm told. Take this job, for instance. Supposing we're indeed going to take some shots of vegetables. What can I conclude from that? Perhaps we're spying for British agriculture, perhaps we're not. I frankly don't know and I don't suppose you're going to tell me, either."

Blakely grunted and asked Hawkins to nevertheless speak a bit about himself. He was sincerely curious about the man, this fellow exile in Paris. Hawkins said that he had crossed the Channel thirty years before in pursuit of a wealthy French woman with whom he had fallen in love during a photoshoot for *Tatler*. She had succumbed rapidly to his charms – "I was a good-looking young man back then, believe it or not" – and he had been invited to move into her home in Neuilly. Their relationship had lasted three months.

"You know how these things are, the fickleness of sentiments, the fleeting nature of passion, and all that stuff," he philosophized. "I soon quit, tired of the endless round of *dîners en ville* with the French bourgeousie. They are *insupportable*, those people. I was made to feel like a butler more than the lady's beau. And to think that they accuse the *English* of being snobs!"

Blakely smiled. "What then?"

"This'll make you laugh. I met a girl, a dancer, from the Folies Bergère in a bar in Pigalle and it turned out that she was passionate about photography and only dreamt of making a living from it. We pooled our modest savings and set up a studio in the Faubourg Saint Denis and haven't looked back. We married and had two kids. It's been a good life."

"And now you're a spy."

"That, by the way, came about because one of the children of the Ambassador at that time hired us to take the pictures of his wedding. I've been freelancing with the embassy ever since. So I get odd, strange trips like this one. It's a real change from my day-to-day life shooting endless family celebrations, that I must say."

Without encouragement, Hawkins settled into the recitation of his life story and droned on about it, on and off, for the next three hours, as Blakely watched the landscape go by, smiling and nodding from time to time. Biarritz did not come too quickly enough.

They picked up the hire car at the station. Blakely took the wheel, proposed to an eager Hawkins to show him a few notable towns and sights, and off they headed into the heartland of the French Basque country on the road towards the Pyrenees.

They stopped in Espelette to admire its house fronts draped with festoons of dried chilli peppers; in Cambo-les-Bains, to visit the mansion and estate built by Edmund Rostand, author of *Cyrano de Bergerac*; and, finally, in Saint-Jean-Pied-de-Port, a popular resting point for pilgrims on the road to the tomb of St. James in Santiago de Compostela before their arduous hike across the mountains into Spain. Here they ate a copious dinner of local sausages, stuffed with pork and beef and red and black peppers, spiced with nutmeg, coriander and caraway, all of it swimming in a dark cream sauce. Great chunks of the sweet and nutty *Ossau Iraty*, the best sheep's milk cheese in the world, rounded off their meal. Well fed indeed, they rolled into Luchère-Les-Bains an hour later and checked into their hotel.

To their mutual horror, they found that the embassy had booked one room only, with twin beds. "This is really taking cost-cutting too far; I'm sorry," Blakely apologized to Hawkins. His embarrassment only increased when the cheeky woman at the reception asked if they wanted the beds pulled together or to be separate. "We'll handle it, don't disturb yourself," Blakely told her irritably as they took the key and went to their room.

"That was a fun day, I thoroughly enjoyed myself, thanks," were Hawkins' last words in the dark before he erupted in raucous snores.

Blakely shook Hawkins out of his sleep at dawn. He would go crazy if he didn't get an hour or two of silent rest alone. His roommate had grunted, coughed, snorted and snored the whole night long.

"Good morning. Now you have to earn your living, Hawkins, I'm afraid," Blakely told him. "First, I want you to go out and take lots of pictures of *Les Bains*, the baths, as many as you can. They're not hard to find. Just ask any of the locals. Then we'll meet at the market at, let's say, ten thirty."

Hawkins went off, covered with cameras, and Blakely returned with relief to his bed.

Three hours later, after a good coffee and a peek at the local newspaper, he found Hawkins sitting on a wall by the market, his head between his hands, staring at his shoes.

"Got the pictures, then?" Blakely asked him.

Hawkins shook his head. "This place is Nutsville, Stephen, an open-air asylum. They're all off their bloody rockers. Every time I asked for '*Les Bains*' they just roared with laughter, pointed at *the ground* and shrugged their shoulders. Was it my accent, or what? *'Où se trouvent Les Bains, s'il vous plaît?'* I don't see anything funny in that, nothing at all. I just don't understand."

Blakely bit his gums so as not to imitate the indigenes. "No matter, Hawkins, it wasn't vital; we'll move on to the second task in our mission. I think we'll have better luck. Now, I want you to move around the market and take a few shots of all the fruit and vegetables. Just a couple will do, nothing fancy. I'll be just behind you."

Hawkins did as he was told, going through all the moves of the professional, testing the light density, fiddling endlessly with his lenses, crouching, climbing up on fruit boxes, trying different angles, taking his shots with the flash and then without. Blakely soon got tired of all this and pushed Hawkins towards the reason they were in Luchère-Les-Bains in the first place. Marie-Pierre and her zucchini.

"Here, I'd like some scenic views, the old couple, the stall, above all the *courgettes* themselves – they're really quite impressive, don't you think? A lot of shots, please. Can I leave you to it? I have a few calls to make. I'll be in one of the cafés on the square over there."

Blakely wandered off and left Hawkins to his work. Sat on the café terrace, he first sent a text message to Ormrod at the Foreign Office: "Mission in progress, looking good. Have not aroused suspicions. Will bring results on Friday, as agreed." Then he called Ruth, telling her that he was with the chessmaster, that all was well, and that he missed and loved her.

After he had been there a little while, he spotted Hawkins staggering across the square in his direction, his arms full of a huge stack of giant zucchini. Half way towards him, one of the vegetables slipped out of his grip and bending down to pick it up, he dropped them all. They rolled like knocked-down skittles across the ground. He reloaded his arms, but before he had collected them all, they fell again.

This is a great way to escape unwelcome attention, thought Blakely, as several of his fellow café clients began to point and laugh heartedly at Hawkins' misfortune. He had seen this kind of behavior many times before and remained amazed that the French hadn't come up with their own word for *schadenfreude* either. They were specialists. Blakely put his coins on the table and went to the photographer's rescue.

They rounded up all the zucchini once more and divided the burden. "What did you buy all these for?" asked Blakely. "I know they're very impressive, but we can't possibly get them all back to Paris."

Hawkins had not had the best morning of his life and did not find the situation amusing. "I couldn't get the shots I wanted," he said. "Too many people and the old couple were getting annoyed. The woman said one or two things in Basque which sounded distinctly unfriendly."

"Gascon," corrected Blakely, "but go on."

"So I thought the easiest thing was to take these back to the hotel room and photograph them in peace and quiet. I've got *all* my equipment there too; I can even take a video if you like."

"Only if they move," suggested Blakely.

"The woman looked incredibly like Ronald Rump, by the way, did you notice?"

"Not at all, I didn't see any resemblance, personally." He prayed that Hawkins would forget his impression. He had already decided to take the memory card from the photographer before the trip was through and to print the results himself.

Two streets from the hotel, they bumped into Mayor Lizarazu.

"My friend! Welcome back! I heard you were in town.

You are true to your word. You *said* you would return. I see that this time you have brought a friend. That's good."

"Monsieur Le Maire, this is Monsieur Hawkins. Monsieur Hawkins, this is Mayor Lizarazu." The Mayor shook hands with a zucchini, since Hawkins didn't have one free.

"So, did you show Mr. Hawkins the baths, *Les Bains*?" asked Lizarazu solemnly. Without waiting for an answer, he walked off, began to shake, and then, howling with joy, he invited them over his shoulder to join him for a drink *Chez Irène* before they left for Paris again, as Blakely explained that they must do at lunchtime.

"What did I tell you? Even the Mayor is a raving lunatic," said Hawkins, shaking his head as he watched Lizarazu wind his way down the street, swept from side to side by his hilarity.

Back at the hotel, Hawkins asked for space and, on Blakely's instruction, arranged the vegetables in various postures, singly and in batches, on the carpet, on the bed, in the shower, on the bureau. He opened his collapsible umbrella, fixed one of his cameras on the tripod, tested the light, changed three times the lenses, and started work. Blakely wanted both black and white and color shots and this doubled the time of everything. He was at it for a full two hours, as Blakely watched and occasionally proffered useless advice about angles and backgrounds. Finally, Hawkins was done *almost* to his satisfaction, which is as good as it gets for photographers who take their work seriously. Blakely urged him to hurry, went to pay the room bill, packed the car, and off they drove towards Biarritz again, stopping only for a few minutes *Chez Irène* to toast the Mayor's health. "I'll be back again," Blakely told him once more.

Blakely and Hawkins unwittingly left behind them the germs of a dubious and rather ribald legend that would feed the rumors and idle chitchat of Luchère-Les-Bains and its citizens for many moons to come. It was the story of two Englishmen, a single booking and a huge quantity of zucchini, unaccountably abandoned in their beds, the bathroom, and on the floor of their hotel room. Hawkins hadn't had time to clear up and thought that this was the maid's job anyhow.

The staff of the hotel ate courgettes for weeks after their departure.

CHAPTER 13

ORMROD AND BLAKELY AT THE CLUB

They met at Ormrod's plush club in Piccadilly.

"Stephen! So nice to see you again. I hope you don't mind this snooty hangout?"

"On the contrary, George, it's marvellous. Peasants like me don't get into these places, usually."

"Goes with the job," Ormrod informed him. "Can't have Foreign Secretaries loitering in dubious bars, can we?"

"How are you settling in to the job, George?" asked Blakely as he sat down. "Must be a real change of pace from DCMS. What's it been like walking into an international crisis? Have any trouble finding Bangistan on a map?"

They both laughed and Ormrod called the waiter for drinks.

"Before we talk about that, tell me about Paris. The French are revolting again, I see. They were preciously close to the Embassy when they smashed up the neighborhood last weekend, weren't they? Good job we're just down the road from the Elysée Palace and that the area was blocked off. What do you think about all that, Stephen, the *gilets jaunes*, the 'yellow vests'? Where's it all going?"

Blakely said that it was anyone's guess, that the movement had surprised and confounded even the most discerning among the scores of political analysts, sociologists, philosophers, anthropologists, psychiatrists, historians, economists, and sundry intellectuals who had rushed to the nearest microphones, cameras, newspapers and magazines to theorize about the events, as they always did in France with phenomena like this, such was the nation's compulsion to analyse absolutely everything to death.

"And you, Stephen, what do you think?"

"When all is said and done, I think this revolt has the same roots as the rise of the populist movements we're seeing all over Europe – and not only Europe, of course. Basically, a deep hatred of the privileged, the elites like us."

"But France has had its extremist, populist parties for a long time," Ormrod intervened. "Le Pen, for example; she and her father have been there for decades."

"This is why the yellow vests are so hard to grasp. They want much more radical and violent change than those parties are promising to deliver. Le Pen and her counterparts on the extreme left have all come into the fold in recent years; they've become institutionalized. Impatient with their electoral failures, they perceived that they'd get nowhere near power unless they were accepted as good *republicans* – a notion the French are very attached to. This *gilets jaunes* revolt caught all the usual extremists napping; they were overtaken by the mob, if you like. The mob doesn't want anything of them, rejects the extremist parties totally as being part of the establishment they're fighting. One of their early leaders even called for the storming of the Elysée, the hanging of the President, the creation of a *people's assembly* and a military coup! They want nothing less than another revolution, actually."

They broke off the discussion for a few moments to order their dinner and more wine. Then Blakely added: "I don't know whether their lack of leadership, lack of a figurehead, the absence of a programme, and their deep hatred of politicians, makes them more, or less, dangerous than the populist parties we see moving into government here and there. Probably less, I think, because they'll finally be crushed by force if they keep going in the direction they've chosen."

"I've been thinking about the populist trends and successes, in Hungary, Poland, Italy, Austria, Brazil and so on, this primal urge to get the tough guys, the authoritarians, in power," said Ormrod. "It's funny, really, all these people voting to elect governments that essentially promise to reduce their rights. That's the worse, for me. People are *knowingly* embracing parties that dream of getting them to march to a single tune, to follow orders. Half of them will end up victims of their own folly, Stephen, if they ever have their way, as has always happened with regimes who incarnate the spirit of repression, regimes that rise to power *against* someone or something, but never for a confident and optimistic cause. I really don't think we're ready quite yet to climb out of the hole we continue to dig for ourselves, our noble human race.

"You know what Churchill said?" Ormrod went on. "'If you want an argument against democracy, go and chat with a voter for five minutes.' It's probably apocryphal, but I'm sure he felt it."

Though Blakely laughed, he countered: "It's all very well saying such things in the comfort and privacy of your gentlemen's club, George, but I don't think that would go down well in a fish and chips shop in Huddersfield. The *'voters'* think that *we're* the problem, not them. We're not in any position at all to mock the people, you know."

"You're becoming a socialist, Blakely. I'll have to bring you home. Too much foreign influence. But you're wrong though. They love me as much in Huddersfield as anywhere else. Even though it's Labour. I can't imagine why."

They sat in silence for several minutes, before Blakely asked, "Bangistan?"

"Certainly, go ahead."

"First of all, George, thanks a lot for giving me the dossier."

"You're the man for the job, my old pal. How did Pickering take it, me stealing one of his stars for a while?"

"No problem at all. 'Good luck. Keep me informed. You'll find me at the Cannes Film Festival if you need me.' That was about it."

Ormrod laughed. "It's about time we brought Sir Edmund home too, I think."

"Thanks also for so readily giving me a free hand to do whatever I want. The trip to the south went smoothly, as I told you, and my ideas are beginning to crystallize. I'm reluctant to explain them to you yet, because I believe that even you will think that I have become certifiable."

"It's always been one of your charms, Stephen, this drive to seek creative, imaginative solutions to insoluble problems. That's why I've given you your head on this one, not only for an old friendship. You're being very mysterious though. I think I'll have to oblige you to give me a clue or two about what exactly it is you're cooking up this time."

Blakely concurred with a nod, asked Ormrod whether anyone was likely to come into their private dining room – "Not unless I pull that," replied the Minister, pointing to a string hanging from the wall behind him – and opened his briefcase. He then set out a number of photographs on an adjoining table. "Take a look at these, George, what do you see?"

The Minister came over and peered, one by one, at the pictures. "So? Rump here, there, and there. And a pile of bombs, or missiles, in those shots. What am I supposed to conclude, Stephen?"

"You're wrong in all cases, George. This," he said, brushing his hand over the three portraits, "is Marie-Pierre Etxeberria; and these are her zucchini in my hotel room shower."

"You're quite right, you're certifiable!" roared Ormrod, looking over the photographs once more. "What on earth are you talking about?"

They ordered coffee and cognac and Blakely recounted his adventures. The holiday break with Ruth; Marie-Pierre and Gaston and their market stall; the mistake made also by his counterpart, Scott, when he had seen the photograph; his return trip to Luchère with Hawkins, who had seen Rump there too, without encouragement; the farce with the zucchini on the village square and the photo session in the hotel.

Blakely then sketched out for the Minister the insane ideas that were beginning to take shape in his mind and that he would like to explore and develop further. All he asked was that Ormrod should give his blessing to take the plan forwards a little and to discuss it in Paris with his American colleague. He would report back after that meeting had taken place.

"It's *your* head, Stephen," Ormrod said after a few minutes reflection. "Even though you're putting mine squarely on the block too. But, as you know well, I couldn't give a damn about that. So, go for it. The whole thing is completely impossible, of course, but it'll be fun while it lasts. I'm intrigued to see how far you can take it."

CHAPTER 14

AT HOME WITH SCOTT

"This is what I like to see – a man in the kitchen!"

"Hi there, Scott. Do you cook too?"

"Not on your sweet life, buddy. I leave that to you docile house husbands."

"I enjoy it," smiled Blakely. "Go and have a drink with Ruth and I'll be along in a moment. I hope you like duck?"

"Love it," said Schurz.

The fowl back in the oven for another half hour, a few minutes later Blakely went and joined his wife and their friend.

"I'm famished, let's start straight away," he told them. "Oysters *gratinées* OK, Scott?"

"Love 'em," said their obliging guest.

They talked a while about nothing in particular, idle chit chat on restaurants they had discovered, their ideas for summer holidays, the riots in France, the chaos around the United Kingdom's departure from Europe, Ruth's latest enthusiasms in literature. They ate their roast duck – "delicious!" enthused Schurz – and then a rich selection of cheeses – "I'm so happy you don't indulge in that ugly British perversion of eating dessert *before* cheese," he said. And then, inevitably, while giving themselves a break before the last course, they came round to the burning issue of the moment.

Ruth launched them on the subject: "So, what are you guys going to do about Bangistan?"

Before Schurz had time to open his mouth, her husband told her: "We're going to prevent Rump from showing up in

Petrobangorski. We can't take the risk."

"You and whose army?" asked Ruth.

"The clandestine army of the night, the soldiers of the shadows, the cloak-and-dagger boys," said Blakely. "In other words ... Scott and me."

"Scott who knows nothing about this," the American told Ruth, grinning. "Go on comrade."

"We have no choice. If we don't stop Rump, we're heading for certain war. We're dealing with madmen, you know, on both sides. The lives of millions are as nothing compared with their egos. They would rather we all die under their bombs than back down and be considered as poltroons in their own deranged minds. Nothing quite like this has ever been seen before, not in the nuclear age, anyhow."

"Yeah, sure," said Schurz. "What's your plan then? You gonna shoot down Air Force One, you Brits?"

"No, we're going to kidnap your President en route. Hold on a moment, I'm going to get the rum babas. Do you like them, Scott?"

"Love 'em. Don't hold back on the rum for me," he shouted after him as Blakely disappeared again into the kitchen. "I'll bring the bottle, don't worry," came the reply.

He returned not with the dessert nor the rum bottle but with a flip chart. "The babas can wait a little more. I've got to tell you the plan," explained Blakely. "I can't keep it to myself any longer. Why don't you take your glasses and sit over there," he proposed, pointing to the sofa. Once ensconced, Schurz said, "Go ahead, Professor, we're all ears."

Blakely described his plan, making notes on the chart. First, the final, all-important objective: "Marie-Pierre Etxeberria – that's the woman in the photograph, Scott – is going to make peace with Akim in Petrobangorski. She'll be switched for Rump on the road to Bangistan."

Ruth and the American simply looked at each other and giggled. "I think we need refills," said Schurz, bringing the wine from the table and sitting down again.

"I've got it all figured out," continued Blakely. "All we need now is to win the hearts and minds and cooperation of a few dozen influential people and we're home and dry."

"Where will the switch take place, Stephen?" asked Schurz to humor him a little more.

"At the G7, of course."

"And whose 'cooperation' are we going to need, you and I, to arrange all this?"

"Your government, most importantly, and France, of course, then Canada, Japan, Germany and Italy, to a lesser degree but at the very highest level. We'll keep the European Union well away from it all, even though their representatives are part of the group. It'll get far too complicated otherwise."

"You didn't mention us, the UK," said Ruth.

"I don't think that'll be any problem, my love. With Ormrod on our side, it'll be a piece of cake. He's got Theresa wrapped around his little finger. The real challenge is to get to the senior figures of the other countries to persuade them that all this can work. We have only six weeks to do it now. I thought that we should start on Friday, Scott, at our regular dinner with the G7 embassy colleagues. Let's feel them out on it."

Schurz continued to play the game, just for the fun of it. "Think about them, Stephen. Sombre-faced, zis-is-not-in-order Schaffelhofer? Sweet Mary, who's in love with Justin and would never drag him into such a business? Gengo Nomura? He's so bloody inscrutable and cautious we'd never get to know whether he was in favor of the plan or not. Giancarlo? It's true that he might go along, disciple of Machiavelli that he is. Who's left? Our Frenchman, of course,

Pierre. Lord only knows which way he might swing; his only concern would be whether it might benefit his career or not – you know how ambitious he is. So, you see Stephen, we're on a hiding to nothing with that bunch. We simply couldn't chance raising the question with them, it would kill the project in the bud."

"You're right, Scott, perhaps a better route would be to go straight to the Foreign Ministers. Maybe I could get Ormrod to make the approach to his colleagues on our behalf."

"Holden's out for a start," said Schurz. "He *wants* things to foul up; he *wants* Rump to go and to fail and to declare war. And we can hardly do without *his* assent and help. He's the main man on this whole Bangistan thing for us. It's even become personal for him, since Akim called him 'a dirty scumbag' in a tweet last week. No, he's only out for full-scale conflict. Forget him."

Blakely sighed, went to the kitchen to fetch the rum babas and the bottle, and summoned them back to the dining table. They ate and drank in silence. Until Ruth said, suddenly:

"The spooks."

"What, my love?" asked Blakely.

"This is a job for the spooks, not the foreign ministers. We need the spymasters in on the plan, the ones who run the external intelligence agencies."

"But how on earth do we get to them?"

"I think I can talk to O'Reilly," ventured Schurz. "He's a close friend of my father. I'm sure I can get the old man to put us in contact."

"The Director of the CIA, isn't he?" asked Ruth.

"That's the guy."

"Would you do it, Scott?" asked Blakely. "Maybe we could go and meet him together. Tell me, though, what's his position on the whole Bangistan business?"

"As far as he can say what he thinks publicly, he's totally

in favor of peace talks and a settlement and adamantly against the use of force."

"Sounds like our man," said Blakely. "He would be an excellent starting point."

"But tell me, Stephen, going back to your plan, how on earth could you pass one man – who, in addition, is a woman – off for another?" asked Ruth. "Isn't that beyond the bounds of credibility?"

"I was waiting for one of you to ask that. There are many precedents of even more prolonged identity subterfuge, you know. Ever heard of Shi Pei Pu?" Schurz, at this point, burst into bellows of self-perpetuating laughter, saying over and over again in a silly, slurred Chinese accent, "Shi Pei Pu … Pei Shi Pu … Pei Pu Shi."

Blakely waited until he had quietened down and then went on, "otherwise known as Mr Butterfly," which just set Schurz off into further rum-fuelled hysterics.

"Well, Shi, who was an opera singer, had an affair with an accountant, Bernard Boursicot, at the French Embassy in Beijing, a sexual relationship that lasted twenty years."

"What's unusual about that?" asked Ruth.

"What's unusual is that Boursicot thought he was in love with and shagging a woman, when Shi turned out twenty years later to be a man – and a spy."

"Can't imagine how that happened," said Schurz, sobering up a little, "but go on."

"And how about Martin Guerre?" Blakely continued. "You've seen the film, I'm sure. Depardieu. The true story of a man who came back from the war, after eight years, walked straight into his home and resumed his relationship with his wife, his family and his friends. Except that he was an impostor, an *identity thief*, who was only exposed when taken to court on another matter altogether. There are countless other cases, all the time. I just thought of another one, the 'cameleon', that Frenchman who spent three months in a family in Texas after convincing them he was their missing son! So, all in all, I think that two days posing as Rump with Akim, who hasn't even met him before, will be child's play."

"How on earth will you get this French peasant to agree to it, though?" asked Schurz.

"I have a plan for that too, my friend, in which you are involved. In the meantime, what do you think about the whole scheme, as I've sketched it out?"

"You're out of your fucking mind, Blakely. Completely nuts. This could get us both the guillotine … In other words – I love it!" said Schurz, leaning across the table and enlacing his friend, giving him mock French kisses on his right, then his left cheek, then the right, then the left, and the right, until Blakely pushed him away and said, "Go home, Mr. Butterfly. And don't forget to get in touch with O'Reilly, if you can. We'll go from there."

*

Six hours later, Blakely was awakened brutally by the insistant ring of his mobile telephone, which he fumbled to find in the dark on his bedside table.

"It's Scott. I just wanted to thank you and Ruth for a beautiful evening."

"Are you fucking crazy, Schurz? Couldn't it have waited for daylight, at least?"

"Just kidding. In fact, I've just talked to O'Reilly. He said he'd be delighted to see his old pal's son again. He remembered me when I was running around his garden in a skirt."

"A skirt?"

"That's what he said. I think he's confusing me with my sister," laughed Schurz, "or maybe Ernest Hemingway."

"*Hemingway*?"

"Yeah. He was brought up wearing dresses."

"Really? That could explain a lot."

They both laughed.

"That's great about O'Reilly, in any case," Blakely told him. "Fantastic. We'll talk tomorrow – today – about details. Good night."

"No, wait. I haven't told you the best of it, Stephen. Believe it or not, he's actually coming to *Paris* in ten days. He and the rest of the G7 spook chiefs have a meeting here to prepare Versailles. He said something about a terrorist threat, or some such. He wasn't clear. Maybe had too much rum with his babas too. He'd like to see me here, anyhow. Counts on me to show him *gai Paree*."

Blakely thanked Schurz profusely for his swift action and said he would ring him in a day or so. "I'm taking you to meet Marie-Pierre," he told him. "It's all part of the plan." And with that, he hung up.

"What was all that about?" mumbled Ruth through the fog of her sleep.

"Just more proof of the existence of God," replied Blakely, turning over and pressing his face against her back.

CHAPTER 15

RETURN TO LUCHÈRE

Blakely called the town hall. He was redirected to *Chez Irène*.

"Monsieur le maire?"

"Oui."

"It's Stephen Blakely here, your English friend."

"Well, this *is* a surprise! What can I do for you, *mon ami*?"

"I need your help, Mayor Lizarazu. I'm coming back to Luchère with another colleague."

"And you want me to arrange for the courgettes to be waiting in your room this time, is that it?"

Blakely heard barely-suppressed giggling on the line and some muffled remarks to someone else in the restaurant.

"Very *drôle*, Mr. Mayor. I see that you are *en forme*, in good humor, today."

"*Comme d'habitude*, as always, my friend."

"Glad to hear it," said Blakely. "You're right that we're coming about the zucchini, the courgettes. We have a proposal to make to Madame Etxeberria, a business deal. I was wondering if you would be able in the next few days to bring us together, in your presence of course. At lunch, perhaps. *J'invite*. It's my invitation."

"Gaston will have to be there, for the translation."

"Of course, of course. That'll make five of us, then. Do you think it's possible?"

"For sure, for sure. We have to wait for market day, though. I don't think I can get Marie-Pierre to travel any other time."

Travel? thought Blakely. Five kilometres into town from her farm is *travel*? It doesn't bode well for persuading her to make a trip to Bangistan, does it?

"Perfect," said Blakely. "I guess that's Friday, as usual?"

"Oui."

"So, let's do this. If you could kindly fix things and ask Irène for a table, at two, I suppose, to allow Marie-Pierre and Gaston to wrap up their stall, we'll be there. We're just coming down for the day, this time. Would you let me know if it's possible? Here, I'll give you my number."

"Not necessary, my friend, not necessary. Marie-Pierre may well be a savage, but in this part of the world, one does not refuse lunch with the Mayor. *C'est un honneur!*"

CHAPTER 16

AS RICH AS MANSU MUSA

"Do you like money, Mister Winkelmeier?" asked the young man.

"No more nor less than the next man, I suppose. It can be useful."

"Great Leader say, certainly less than *him*. He say he couldn't live in that miserable shack you call an Embassy, for starters."

The interpreter grinned. He was one of the President's regular staff, a member of the special Twitter team, and knew Winkelmeier a little.

The Ambassador was back in the Presidential Palace to prepare the terrain for Rump's visit and negotiations. Holden had called him earlier with orders for what he should convey about the US position, underlining twice that the White House would absolutely not accept his personal absence in Petrobangorski. Winkelmeier didn't trust the Secretary of State at all, knew he was lying about his own case, and decided to tone down the demands. Rump could say what he wanted on the day, whatever crossed his mind – and would do precisely that, in any case.

"Great Leader ask if you know who richest man in world, in history?"

"Jeff Bezos?" ventured Winkelmeier.

"Great Leader say he never heard of him."

"Bill Gates?"

"Never heard of him."

"Mark Zuckerberg?"

"Never heard of him."

"Great Leader ask, 'you give up?'"

"Yes, yes, of course."

The President mumbled another name.

"Mansu Musa," said the translator.

"Never heard of him," said Winkelmeier. "Sorry."

Hakim Akim readied to spit, thought twice about it, and instead scowled. He got to his feet, came round his desk, walked past the Ambassador's chair, and began to pace up and down his voluminous office, speaking all the while. He waved his arms to the left and to the right, as though sowing seeds on his marble floor; he gasped and laughed and roared and from time to time shouted, beating his fist on his chest; occasionally, he cupped his hands before him, closed his eyes and bowed. The translator scribbled frenetically on his notepad, flicking over the pages and nodding to himself constantly.

Winkelmeier sat and watched this animated spectacle, which lasted a good ten minutes, catching only the words 'Mansu Musa', which seemed to coincide with the breast thumps. Finally, the President fell silent and returned behind his bureau. He motioned to the interpreter to do his job.

"Great Leader say Musa King of Mali, long, long, long time ago. His empire very, very big, half Africa. Musa had much, much, much gold, more than any man before or since. All his soldiers, even his slaves, dress in gold and silk clothes. Musa he went to Mecca with caravan of sixty thousand men, hundreds of camels carrying gold. Right through Egypt, King throw gold coins to people who watch him go past on his road."

At this point, the interpreter struggled to decipher his notes, turning the pages back and forth to pick up the thread again, but Akim signalled to him to shut up anyhow. The President only added, for translation again:

"I want to be as rich, more rich, than Mansu Musa. Then I also will go to Mecca, make *hajj*, throw gold at Arabs. This is my dream."

Winkelmeier suspected that the United States of America was right there and then being set up to foot the bill for Akim's voyage and other fantasies. The President's next questions rather confirmed his conjectures.

"How much gold you have, Winkelmeier?"

"Me, personally?"

"No, your country."

"About eight thousand tons, I think."

"What's that worth, you know?"

"Somewhere around three hundred billion dollars, I would say."

Learning the sum, which he checked twice with the interpreter, Akim grimaced. "Is that all? King Masu spend more than that on his chickens! You very poor country."

"We have other riches, Your Excellency, don't worry about us," said Winkelmeier with a smile.

The paucity of gold in America seemed to make Akim fleetingly unhappy and impatient. He invited Winkelmeier to "come to the point" and tell him what Rump had in mind for their upcoming negotiations.

"With pleasure, President. Please note very carefully what I'm saying," he told the interpreter, "and translate word for word as we go along."

And turning back to Akim: "President Rump's long-term objective, his ardent desire, is to see a nuclear-free world," lied Winkelmeier, nodding to the interpreter to communicate this solemn aspiration.

Akim laughed. "Long term? That next week for Rump, no?"

"He joking, Mr. Ambassador," the young man clarified.

Akim went on, though. "Nuclear free? You scrap missile

agreement with Russians; you tear up nuclear deal with Iran. We supposed to trust you?"

"Those agreements were flawed, Mr. President …"

"What 'flawed' mean?" the interpreter interrupted him.

"Unbalanced, defective, ambiguous, ineffective, unproductive. They simply weren't working. We tried to play by the rules and Russia and Iran took advantage of us." Right out of the State Department's directive to diplomats on how to extricate oneself from any debate on these perfidies. Winkelmeier was proud of himself.

The young man struggled and stumbled over all the Ambassador's complex words and was, in any case, soon interrupted again by Akim, who barked two or three sentences in reply.

"Great Leader, he say cut the bullshit, Winkelmeier. We have nuclear weapons and missiles; you have nuclear weapons and missiles. You demand we give up ours; you keep yours. What kind of deal is that? Big joke, no?"

"We had them before you," said the Ambassador limply.

"Not much before," said Akim. "We have them for two generations, gifts to my family from Russian brothers."

Winkelmeier knew very well that no credible argument at all could justify why some nations continued to possess the ultimate weapon and others were told they couldn't. One could squabble and philosophize about it until doomsday if one wanted to; it was just so. The powerful wrote the rules, that was all. It had always been thus and always would be. If everybody could be open and clear about that, it would considerably simplify international relations in general and his job in particular.

Akim sat and laughed to himself. He had gone through much misery and mental torture after his miscreant half-wit of a brother had confessed the great secret to him. He had been terrified that they would be unable to keep the secret to themselves, that it would somehow get out and lead to their humiliation, disgrace, defeat and certain destitution. But the days had gone by as always, as they had the habit of doing. And right now, the American Ambassador was sitting in front of him discussing in all seriousness the dismantling of Bangistan's completely inexistent weapons arsenal. Akim left him to drone on. The details had no importance any longer, after all. They would of course pretend to do whatever Rump wanted. The only question was the price. If they didn't have five hundred billion dollars in gold to give him (this was the nice round figure he had been thinking about all along), they would have to negotiate the transfer of other commodities. He would accept a certain part in cash, of course.

From what Akim knew of the American President – based on reports from Yogi's intelligence services, which had copied everything out of the New Yorker magazine – he thought that they would get on very well together. When Rump didn't like people or they contradicted him, he fired them. Akim was no different, though he usually removed people in a more permanent fashion. Rump wanted walls set up around his country; this was precisely the Akim family tradition. While Rump was trying to stop people from getting into America, he, Hakim, was trying to stop them from getting out of Bangistan. The American thought that everyone was out to screw him – China, Russia, in particular. Akim had come to the same conclusion, but he was screwing them first, cheating on the gas bills, for instance. Rump had so far only dabbled in despotism? Akim was informed that more and more people in America were embracing his points of view on this question and that a dictatorship would in time come naturally. It was all very reassuring. This was a man he could no doubt deal with.

Left only with tweets and rocks to throw at Rump, Akim nevertheless shared his demands with Winkelmeier.

"We ready to stop tests, underground explosions, missile launches, destroy nuclear warheads, eliminate uranium plants, close mines. We simply destroy everything, that easiest."

"That's excellent," Winkelmeier intervened.

"In exchange for this," Akim continued, "we want complete withdrawal of your nuclear weapons from Europe and *very, very* big help develop our poor country."

"I think it's fair to tell you, Your Excellency, that the President is extremely well disposed to discuss your second suggestion, but I don't think he's in any position to comply with your first request. It's not anything we have against you, you understand. It's just that we have a long-standing commitment to protect our friends and allies in Europe against any unreasonable incursion into their territories, by the Russians for example."

"You not move ass for Crimea or Donbass, I see," Akim smiled. "Putin did what he want there, no?"

"Maybe yes, maybe no," conceded Winkelmeier. "But I think Ukraine was a special, unique case."

"Maybe you say same thing when Russia occupy Georgia, Winkelmeier? They're still there, you know, in South Ossetia and Abkhaz. And your 'red line' in Syria, my friend? Chemical weapon. What happen there? Nothing, Russians still laughing about it. You see, Ambassador, your word and your 'protection' not so good, I think. I want deal where you not cheat me."

Winkelmeier could only sigh and say, rather pathetically, "It's all very complex, I know."

Akim was pleased with himself for occupying briefly the moral high ground. Even dictators needed to do that from time to time. These negotiations would go well, he was sure of it. He would destroy what didn't exist ... including a little uranium enrichment that they were struggling with anyhow.

In the process, he would obtain enough riches to follow in the hallowed footsteps of King Mansu Musa.

CHAPTER 17

HOW AKIM FELL IN LOVE WITH MARIE-PIERRE'S ZUCCHINI

They took the same route as Blakely had followed on the Hawkins escapade, though they didn't stop for the peppers, *Cyrano*, the pilgrims or the sausages. They were in a hurry. As consolation, Schurz admired the green, fertile landscapes, the stone houses and walls, the ubiquitous sheep grazing on the steep, almost perpendicular hillsides – "What equilibrists, fantastic," he said.

"It's a special Basque sheep variety, actually," said Blakely. "They breed them with hind legs longer than their forelegs. Then, while they are still lambs, they train them to graze *uphill*."

"That's unusual," said Schurz.

"Indeed, but it's the fruit of many catastrophes," said Blakely. "In the past, if one of them stumbled and fell, the whole flock would follow, tumbling down into the valley and breaking their necks. You know how sheep are."

Schurz was silent, thinking about this ingenuity of the clever Basques. Then Blakely asked him: "Any last questions about our meeting? It's all pretty simple, I think. Don't forget that the Mayor, Lizarazu – you'll adore him – speaks pretty good English, so no dodgy side remarks."

"You're sure you didn't tell them what you do for a living, that you're a diplomat?"

"Quite sure, not even the Mayor. You know the French. They never ask your business, your profession, where you were educated or how much you earn. It's not polite. One waits for a man to give such information, if he wants to. So, I don't think we'll raise any suspicion at all announcing we're in the international fruit and vegetable export trade. All my behavior on the last trip pointed towards some such activity, in any case."

Two hours out of Biarritz, they drove into Luchère-Les-Bains and pulled up outside *Chez Irène*.

"Just one more question, Stephen, before we go in. You were pulling my leg about the sheep weren't you?"

"Only your hind leg. You're uncharacteristically slow this morning, Schurz."

They both laughed. "One last, last thing, Scott: take the *ttoro*, Irène's fish stew, it's quite outstanding."

Lizarazu and the Etxeberrias were waiting for them; they had already started drinking. When the Mayor saw them enter, he gestured to Marie-Pierre and Gaston to get to their feet and hastened to the entrance to greet them.

Schurz just had time to whisper, "Oh my stars and garters! Holy Moses! It's Rump. Jesus! What a likeness," before Lizarazu was shaking Blakely's hand with great vigor while asking the American: "Welcome to Luzère, has my friend shown you the …?," at which point, Blakely cut in, laughing: "No, I haven't, Mr. Mayor. Don't you have any *other* jokes?" Lizarazu laughed in turn. "Yes, indeed! Did you hear about the two Englishmen in a hotel room with twenty kilo of courgettes? *This* has become our favorite new joke in Luzère!"

The banter stopped there. They all turned to see the Etxeberrias staring at them coldly beside the table on the other side of the room and walked over. Lizarazu made the introductions, half in French, with a little Basque seasoning, and, out of politeness to the foreigners and to show off his linguistic talents to two of his citizens, half in English. Gaston translated a few of the words into Gascon for the still unsmiling Marie-Pierre. And this was the way of it for the next two hours. English, French, Basque and Gascon, back and forth in every combination.

Once they were settled in and had ordered, Stephen Blakely embarked on a long recital of the insane proposition that had brought him back to town. As they might know – they didn't, of course – news of Marie-Pierre's outstanding, delicious zucchini had not only reached the Elysée Palace, but the vegetable itself had graced the President's table and palate when it had been served at one of his lunches for key foreign diplomats. It had been the talk of the occasion! The British and American ambassadors, in particular, had remarked on it, had called the chef, and had demanded to know his suppliers. He told them he had been exploring the Basque country one day and had chanced upon the zucchini at the Luchère market.

Gaston and Marie-Pierre exchanged words. "We don't remember any such chef," said the man.

"Of course not. How could you?" replied Blakely. "He shops incognito – he doesn't go around shouting that he runs the Elysée kitchens. They have to be cautious, you know, a little secretive. Who knows? Someone might want to poison the President!" This explanation appeared to satisfy the suspicious Etxeberrias, so Blakely took up his tale again.

"To cut a long story short, the British ambassador sent his chef here too after that! Only the best for him, you know. And he in turn served your zucchini to one of *his* guests – the Paris consul of the People's Popular Democratic Republic of Bangistan. Seeing how wild this gentleman became about the *exquisite* taste of your vegetable, the ambassador gave him a zucchini as a parting gift. And do you know what?" asked Blakely, pausing for translations and a response.

"No," came in unison from the three Luchèrois.

"On the consul's next visit to Petrobangorski – that's the capital – he took it with him and presented it personally to his President. Yes. *Your* zucchini, after its long voyage, ended up on the table of none less than His Excellency Hakim Akim."

Gaston had lost the plot somewhere along the line and asked Lizarazu, in Basque, what the hell the lunatic was talking about. He was willing to translate for Marie-Pierre, of course, but he had to understand something first. The Mayor asked him for patience. He would get to the bottom of this tale from the Arabian Nights.

"My friends do not know what you talking about, Blakely. I am not sure that I do either, to tell you the truth. Please get to the point and then work backwards, it will be easier for us. We have never heard of this place you talk about – 'Bang ... what?' – and why it should concern us."

"Bangistan, Mr. Mayor. It's on the eastern border of Russia and the western border of China. The point is that President Akim has decided that in future he wants to eat *only* the Etxeberria's zucchini and no other. And eventually to have the people of his nation grow them too. He generally gets his way. Anyhow, his consul in Paris went back to the British ambassador to ask for the origin of the excellent *courgettes* he had eaten and taken away as a present. And the embassy staff came to us, The Blakely-Schurz Export Company, to take over and arrange the whole business. Voilà! We propose ourselves as your facilitators in a thriving, new business development for you – zucchini for Bangistan!"

Lizarazu translated into Basque; Gaston translated the Basque into Gascon; Marie-Pierre's answer needed no translation. She shook her head from side to side and repeated, "*Nani, nani, nani, nani, nani.*"

"You give it a shot, Schurz, old partner," sighed Blakely.

"Sure. Please ask your wife if there is something on your

farm that you lack, perhaps, or something that you need to replace," Schurz proposed to Gaston. The old man complied and there was a clearly tense exchange of words.

"Marie-Pierre says that you should mind your own business if you know what's good for you."

Blakely and the Mayor laughed at this Gascon witticism. Schurz persisted with his line of questioning.

"Maybe you could use some refrigeration, a cold store? If you had one of those, you could freeze your courgettes after the harvest and sell them all year round, even in winter."

Another exchange took place between the couple. Marie-Pierre seemed to thaw just slightly.

"You are not so stupid as you look, says my wife."

"It's funny, I was telling him exactly the same thing recently," Blakely chipped in. He was rewarded by a kick in his shins under the table.

"Perhaps you need a new tractor or seeding machine, or harvester?" Schurz continued relentlessly. "You'll need the best equipment if you're going to increase production and provide Bangistan with the kind of quantities that President Akim has in mind."

Here, Gaston made his own contribution to the discussion. "It's true, Marie-Pierre breaks her back with those damn courgettes – she does most of the work by hand. I have told her many times we should either get good machines or try and live simply off the sheep and the cheese. But we don't have the money for such things and at our age no one wants to lend it to us. We most certainly need a new tractor; the old one is breaking down all the time."

It was the longest speech that Mayor Lizarazu had ever heard Etxeberria make, and he patted him fondly on the back. Yes, he had every reason to be proud of Gaston. Now it was his own turn to talk.

"Mr. Blakely and Mr. Schurz. Why do you speak of these fine things in front of my friends? They cannot afford them. Yes, they are in difficulty, but I do not think that to sell a few zucchinis to this Arab is going to change anything. It just complicates their lives, non?"

"He's not Arab, Mr. Mayor, rather Turkic or Tartar or something of the sort," said Blakely. "But that's *sans importance*. The point is that his country, Bangistan, is poor and undeveloped – though it's said that President Akim himself is rather affluent – and also quite unstable. It has recently become important to all of us in the West in a ... *strategic* sense. You perhaps don't follow international news very much" – "you're right", Lizarazu broke in soberly – "but, well, we are now all anxious to help the nation create a new era of prosperity and peace."

"And that means," Schurz intervened without invitation, "that some of the foreign governments we work with are willing to invest money in the future of Bangistan – most notably the British." Blakely returned the kick in the shins.

"And how does that concern the Etxeberrias?" asked the Mayor.

"Because these investments, these development aid programmes, also have an important tranche of support available for the suppliers of the products necessary to give the Bangistan economy this new start."

"Like zucchini?" suggested the Mayor.

"Indeed, indeed," said Blakely and Schurz in unison.

"I will explain to our friends," said the Mayor. And this he did, at considerable length, in Basque - translated by Gaston for Marie-Pierre - so the foreigners couldn't follow. The Etxeberrias became visibly agitated, but in a positive way, they thought. Each time one or other of them made an objection or asked for a clarification, Lizarazu confidently waved his arms, gushed enthusiastically, and reduced them to silence and contemplation. He thinks he's found his new *Bains*, Blakely said to himself.

When he was quite done with his persuasions, the Mayor told Blakely and Schurz that a deal was quite possibly conceivable, with his further help and advice, of course, and perhaps a little incentive, and that they could count on him to bring it to fruition. If the support they suggested were to be timely, Luchère's first zucchini could be on their way to the Arabs in a couple of months, with much bigger quantities to follow once their land had been cultivated properly and *mechanically*.

All this called for a new round of drinks and a toast. "To prosperity and friendship!" proposed the Mayor. Everyone looked happy, for the first time since they had gathered.

"And the trip?" Schurz asked Blakely.

"Another time, Scott. Yes," he said, turning to Lizarazu and the Etxeberrias, "one of us or another representative of the company will be back soon for further, very concrete discussions on the way forward. I'll be in touch."

As they got up to leave, Mayor Lizarazu took Blakely in his arms and kissed him on both cheeks – twice, actually. He also shook Schurz's hand vigorously.

"Very nice to meet you, Englishman."

"American," said Schurz.

"Let's not start that again, Mr. Mayor," laughed Blakely. And they were gone. Turning to salute Irène at the door, they saw Lizarazu and the Etxeberrias already plunged anew in an intense and spirited discussion.

"Why didn't ..." Schurz began as they drove out of town.

"I thought it was just too much for a first discussion," said Blakely. "Psychology. I think it would have scared the wits out of Marie-Pierre if we told her she had to go and meet Akim to sign the contract, even just as a formality. They'll be time for that. We must first really seal their engagement in this whole business."

"Yes, maybe you're right."

"In any case, thanks a lot Scott. It was decisive that you came in when you did about the machinery. Up until then, they didn't look in the slightest bit interested about what I was talking about. How do you know so much about agricultural equipment?"

"My family are farmers."

"Good Lord, I didn't know that."

"Yup. I was brought up on a farm in Iowa. I'm just a yokel at heart."

"That, I had noticed."

"Ha! How about a farm joke?"

"Why not?"

Schurz began laughing. "Two farmers, Bill and Burt, are sitting on the porch one day insulting each other as usual. 'You're so incredibly dumb, Bill, you don't even know how to write.' 'Oh yes I does,' he says. 'Yeah? Alright Einstein, spell 'farm' for me.' Bill racks his brains to come up with an answer, but has to admit defeat. 'Bet you can't spell it neither, wise guy,' he tells Burt. 'Of course I can!' says Burt. 'Now you'll see how dumb you *really* are. It's in the song!' 'What song?' says Bill. 'I'll tell you: 'Old Macdonald had a *farm*, E-I-E-I-O.'"

They laughed themselves stupid over this and other silly stories half the way back to Paris.

Later that day, at Ormrod's bidding and after a call from Blakely, Sally at the Foreign Office endeavored to contact Ambassador Pickering. She finally tracked him down, thanks to a bellboy, at a very exclusive party in the Majestic Hotel in Cannes.

Sir Edmund extricated himself, not without difficulty and regret, from a coterie of stunning young actresses he was regaling with stories of his youthful hunting parties with the Queen, most particularly the time he famously shot a tiger in Kathmandu practically under Her Majesty's nose.

The Ambassador apologized in advance for a *very brief* absence, went up to his room, opened his computer, and sent an email to the procurement officer at the embassy. "Buy Blakely a tractor – any model he asks for. And don't ask why."

CHAPTER 18

THE PLOT TAKES SHAPE

He arrived two days before the meeting. After all, this was Paris, and even a CIA Director was entitled to a little fun and recreation from time to time. O'Reilly had only two professional obligations: he had promised to meet the son of his old friend Schurz; he must brief his French counterpart on current American objectives with regard to the most important questions of the day, chief among them their latest policy in the Bangistan crisis – provided that he could figure it out, of course.

Rump, O'Reilly, Holden and Zebriski had met again shortly before his departure from Washington. Ambassador Winkelmeier's latest report from Petrobangorski still hadn't come in and the meeting had thus been brief. Intelligence, such that it was in that part of the world, had picked up nothing of interest. No troop movements, no suspicious earth tremors, no heightened telecommunications activity, no more missile launches and, most importantly, nothing new from @bestdespot on Twitter. To all appearances, the situation was frozen. They thus agreed to go about their business as usual, promising to keep in touch, hour-by-hour if necessary.

Just about to board the Paris flight at Dulles, O'Reilly was handed an envelope by one of his agents based at the airport. He opened it once the plane was in the air and he had a drink in his hand. It contained a cable from Winkelmeier, in the Ambassador's usual long-winded and slightly obscure style.

"Akim reiterates his agreement to rendezvous in Petrobangorski."

I should damn well hope so, O'Reilly said to himself. He doesn't know his luck. He read on:

"No more missile tests, detonations or tweets if America behaves itself, he says."

Cheeky son-of-a-bitch, thought O'Reilly.

"Secretary Holden's presence totally unacceptable. He won't budge on this."

Not such a bad guy after all, that Akim, O'Reilly laughed, raising his glass in a solitary toast.

"Akim demands discretion. No foreign reporters allowed in to Bangistan (they don't have any of their own); no statements unless deal concluded."

Rump won't like that at all, O'Reilly told himself. Great deeds done in secret might as well not exist, as far as he was concerned.

"He still insists that our nuclear arms should be pulled out of Europe – but happily doesn't mention those we have elsewhere."

Happily? Are you kidding us Winkelmeier? This Akim is really not so stupid. He knows we won't destroy our own missiles, but Rump might well just concede a withdrawal from Europe, who knows? Weakening and scaring the Europeans would be right up his alley, O'Reilly was sure of it.

"Much talk also about gold. We don't have nearly enough, apparently. Certainly not as much as King Musa."

King *who*? You're losing your grip Winkelmeier, out there in the wilderness, thought O'Reilly. It sometimes happens to some of my agents too, he reflected. "It's not the moment to go rogue on us, Ambassador," muttered O'Reilly, as though he were talking to him there and then.

"Not enough to make a trip with his army to Mecca and to throw coins at Arabs along the way," O'Reilly read on, raising his eyebrows and shaking his head in disbelief.

The insane Winkelmeier came to the actual point of his encounter with Akim right at the end of the three pages:

"To summarize the situation as I see it: President Akim is will-

ing to give up everything, his nuclear warheads, his missile development programme, his tests, his uranium enrichment plants, if the price is right. If President Rump could just get him to drop the European withdrawal demand, something that might require much more money on the table, of course, then I think a deal and permanent peace are possible."

As O'Reilly ordered his foie gras, chose lightly-grilled scallops with truffle sauce as a main course, and settled in for a fine French lunch, the harbinger of many to come in the next few days, back in Washington Rump ordered Holden and Zebriski to come to the White House to discuss Winkelmeier's brief.

"Who the hell is Musa?" the President greeted them.

"I looked him up," said Holden. "The King of Mali."

"And where the hell is Mali?"

"In Africa, Sir," said Zebriski.

"Do we trade with Mali?" asked Rump. "Are we in deficit with Musa? I bet he's screwing us like everybody else, isn't he?"

Zebriski explained gently that the gentleman in question had been dead for seven hundred years and therefore was no longer a real problem or a threat for the United States.

"Just as well for him," said the President, who was suffering from severe Akim tweet embargo withdrawal symptoms and in need, rapidly, of someone else with whom he could get mad, a new adversary for his insults and attacks.

Holden, who was grief-stricken to learn that he still couldn't go on the trip, restrained himself from spitting on Winkelmeier's report and advised President Rump to go into the Petrobangorski meeting with "guns blazing," an expression that made Zebriski wince.

"We can't let this bozo push us around any longer, Mr. President," he said boldly. "This isn't a conversation around the campfire. Akim needs to be taught a lesson. We're not asking, we are demanding that he abandon his arms programme. Maybe, as a little incentive, we could fire a missile right over his fucking head – into the Kalimari Mountains, for example. Without threats, no concessions."

"That isn't a threat, it's an act of war," said Zebriski

"I don't know, Holden," said Rump. "Sure, I'd be a hero in Alabama for twenty-four hours if I fired your missile. But I don't think there are many other upsides. No, we must appear to be looking for peace. We have no other option. Akim has got us by the balls and won't let go until we make a deal. It's a damn shame that Russia didn't take its nukes back, but they didn't and there's nothing we can do about that now."

Holden knew when to give up, knew when the fat lady had sung. He wouldn't be on the trip to influence the outcome and had better get used to it. Nothing he could do or say could any longer dynamite the deal in advance, either. Rump was on his own now. God bless America.

*

They were in Harry's Bar, shouting at each other above the din of their expatriate compatriots and assorted French americanophiles who loved the busy, noisy atmosphere and yearned for New York.

O'Reilly suggested they go somewhere more French, *more civilized*, as he put it. "And call me Dan, if you wouldn't mind, son," he instructed.

Schurz took him across the river to the hotel l'Hôtel in the Rue des Beaux-Arts, where Oscar Wilde famously died beyond his means and after a duel with the wallpaper. The bar was silent and most discrete.

After a few, confused childhood reminiscences, memories of visits to O'Reilly's home, and some intimate talk about his father, Schurz asked whether he would mind if his friend Stephen from the British Embassy joined them. Blakely had some interesting ideas that O'Reilly might like to hear. The

Director said he would be happy for it, and ten minutes later Blakely showed up. He had been hanging around Saint Germain waiting for Schurz's call.

O'Reilly was delighted to learn that the British had given Blakely the Bangistan talks preparation assignment in advance of Versailles. "Not that I think the talks have any purpose at all," he told him, "except to brief all you guys on what President Rump thinks he will propose when he meets Akim. Even we're not clear about that, incredible as it might sound." They all laughed knowingly.

"Can I take it we're all talking out of school?" asked Blakely. "To the extent that our duties and responsibilities allow it, of course," he added gravely, suddenly reminding himself that he was actually sitting there with the most powerful spy in the world, for Christ's sake, the one guy who possessed *all* the secrets.

"What would you like to know?" asked O'Reilly, smiling.

"Right … Who killed JF Kennedy?"

"Your friend's funny, Scott," the CIA Director said without malice.

"Quite a wit, indeed," said Schurz drily.

"No, seriously, what's your take on Bangistan, Sir?"

"I'm Dan, Stephen."

"Great, fine Dan."

"We in the CIA don't have any politics and don't promote any policies in the public sphere, you understand that?"

"Yes, of course."

"We are there to seek and provide information, the facts, to the President, and to assess them if he asks us to."

"Quite."

"So, Bangistan. I guess I won't be saying anything that isn't public knowledge if I admit that my agency wasn't on its toes with that any more than anyone else. The Akims seemed to be minding their own business and not troubling anybody, so we didn't waste any resources on them. In any case, it would have been damn difficult to find out what was going on, so closed off is that place. I think the *Times* – New York, that is – got it about right when they called it the 'forgotten Stan'."

"I think we were all guilty," said Blakely to be agreeable.

"Anyhow, you know what happened. The first tweets, then counter-tweets, counter-counter-tweets, insults, threats, and finally that Caspian missile test that woke us all up to the reality. Bangistan had been harboring nuclear arms and an intercontinental ballistic missile capability that no one knew about. Thanks to the Russians, it turns out, who left them behind when they pulled out. For twenty-eight years they do nothing, keep their noses clean; our President threatens to silence their tweeting, then boom, we're overnight in a war crisis."

O'Reilly shook his head sadly and called the waiter for another round of drinks.

"And what now?" Blakely pushed him.

"Well, there aren't a dozen different options, of course, for American action. It's not a secret that it's split the administration down the middle. The hawks want Bangistan wiped off the map or, alternatively, invaded – the Akims would be a pushover, it's true, *but only if they didn't get to the nuclear button first*. The others say that's precisely a gamble we can't make and that we must in some way or another come to a peaceful agreement, one that takes away any risks at all for the foreseeable future. President Rump is with the second group. He's seen what happened to previous Presidents who went down the road of conflict and war. None of them since Roosevelt have come out shining, to say the least; all of them have been tarnished, not to mention that we've lost practically all the wars in which we've engaged ever since."

"Well, you won the Cold War," said Blakely to cheer him up.

"I like you, young man," said O'Reilly, "you're damn right we did – and without firing a shot! Thanks in large part, I would say, to the CIA, to my predecessors and to our agents, and their tireless efforts to sap the strength of the enemy and to destroy it from within. I once met Putin, you know, in East Germany, when he was a KGB agent."

"Good Lord!," said Blakely, "please do tell us about it."

O'Reilly needed no encouragement and readily told his story, which had developed and changed over the years and become, to put it kindly, a little *embellished*. He and the present Russian President had practically decided, man to man, to cooperate on the downfall of the Soviet Union.

But it was time to go on to another bar, and get something to eat, so they called a taxi and went off to the Rosebud in Montparnasse, where Dominique obligingly found them an isolated corner table while Billie Holiday sang *Prelude to a Kiss* softly in the background.

He hadn't exactly been stiff that evening in the company of his new friends, but O'Reilly was certainly loosening up. As a seasoned spy, he could not, of course, allow himself to become *too* tipsy, but he had good resistance to alcohol and readily agreed to try the very *peaty* smoky martini, a house speciality, before they ate.

Blakely hadn't drunk nearly enough. Not, in any case, a sufficient quantity to embolden himself for his mission. He drank scotch right through his chili con carne, while the others, more reasonably, sipped their wine.

He could probably have me shanghaied right here and now, thought Blakely. A screech of tires, footsteps on the pavement, two or three agents bustling him out of the bar. In twenty-four hours, he'd be in Guantanamo Bay wearing an orange jumpsuit. Jesus, I didn't think that my nerves would let me down to this extent. One last try to situate O'Reilly politically on Bangistan, he promised himself, particularly since Schurz was giving him more and more urgent looks, winks and slight shifts of the head.

"So, Dan," he resumed. "I understand that your functions don't permit you to express political opinions, that's clear. But the line between *assessing* a situation and suggesting a course of action, a policy, which you have said is not within your remit, is a rather fine one, don't you think? It would help Britain a lot, it would provide precious guidance to our Prime Minister, if we knew from such a veteran expert as yourself what you think is the ideal way forward and what you expect, as things stand, will be the outcome."

"Look guys, this has to stay between us. I never said what I'm going to say, right?"

They nodded eagerly.

"Firstly, I never wanted the President to go to Petrobangorski in the first place and still don't. It seems like madness to me. I'm far too loyal to say anything negative about Rump, but he simply isn't prepared for these matters. Negotiating to build a tower block in Manhattan just ain't the same thing as deciding war or peace with a cunning, deceitful and possibly psychopathic third world dictator who, in addition, possesses nuclear bombs and the means to deliver them to our doorsteps." He paused and asked for another bottle of wine.

Blakely and Schurz held their breath.

"You know, I don't even care that much what he gives away to Akim if that son-of-a-bitch really does intend, in exchange, to destroy his entire arsenal, as our man in Bangistan informs us. So, we pull our nukes out of Europe? We can always ship them back. But who's to guarantee anything at all? Here we have two very temperamental and volatile men with very … very … *affirmed* egos and reputations for … for … *iconaclastic*, yes, that's the word, *iconaclastic* behavior. Believe me, guys, anything could happen, really anything, including a complete bust up and missiles shooting off all over the goddam place."

"War or peace decided on a throw of the dice. However did we get here?" Schurz said to no one in particular.

Now was the moment.

"Unless, of course, President Rump never makes it to Petrobangorski," said Blakely.

"Aside from an act of God – not being irreligious, or anything – that's a pious hope, I'm afraid, young man," said O'Reilly.

"Let me show you something, Dan."

Blakely reached inside his jacket and brought out a stack of photographs. Only headshots, this time. He didn't want to confuse matters with the dress.

"Hail to the Chief," said O'Reilly, shuffling through the pictures. "Do you always carry these with you?" handing them back to Blakely. "A fan?" he smiled.

"This isn't President Rump."

O'Reilly took the photographs back from him and looked at each of them again, more slowly this time. He said nothing.

"This is his clone. A French peasant woman. Scott and I have met her. We think that she should go to Bangistan in Rump's place."

As O'Reilly had told them and as they all accepted, the CIA did not involve itself in politics, except those of other nations, of course; that was its code, its guiding principle, its honor. The good men and women who worked for the agency were not especially interested in them either. Yes, they worked, tirelessly, in pursuit of the ambitions and objectives set by their political masters. But they did not have to embrace these ends philosophically; they were a matter of indifference to them. If this is amoral, so be it, more than one agent had said to him- or herself at one time or other. And, after all, if in weak moments, moments of doubt, they needed a justification for their activities, they could always turn to patriotism, the love of country, and similar vacuous sentiments.

The rewards of spying were to be found quite elsewhere than in politics, elsewhere than in advancing this or that cause. They lay, above all, in the extraordinary pleasure of intrigue, of subterfuge, of guile, of secrecy, of danger, of *outwitting the enemy*. Yes, in signing up for the CIA, a very public secret service, its officers knew that they would work for an oxymoron, but this was a small price to pay. They were of course rather ashamed, wounded in their professional pride – particularly the older generation – that their masters had created *websites*, pages on Facebook, Twitter and Instagram accounts, had hired communication directors. But they found their consolation for this joke and farce of publicizing the actions of a covert organization in being able to rejoice over the extent to which they could pull the wool over everyone's eyes in these places too.

Without displaying emotion or expressing any judgement, Dan O'Reilly asked Stephen Blakely to share what he had on his mind. Empathy, real or feigned, together with attentiveness, were a central feature of every agent's behavioral training and methodology, and the CIA Director had mastered both a long time ago. He let Blakely speak, without interruption, of doppelgängers, of zucchini, of tractors and seeding machines, of fruit and vegetable exports, of abduction, of substitution, of bluff of a magnitude rarely seen in international affairs, of peace.

"You're pretty devious for an idealist," joked O'Reilly, when Blakely had come to the end of his story.

"Idealist?"

"That's how Scott described you, in any case."

"I've been called worse things," said Blakely, smiling.

"That's quite a tale you've told. What does your Ambassador think about it?"

"He doesn't know."

"Really? Does anyone? Apart from the three of us."

"Yes, the Foreign Minister in London. He's a friend, too."

"And?"

"He likes it a lot. He gave me my head."

"On a platter?"

Blakely laughed.

"He has a lot of confidence in me, wants to see how far I can take the idea."

"And you thought that I might help? That I would betray my President, betray the United States of America? You're proposing treason, young man, you're aware of that? In the States, it's still a capital crime, you know."

"I've thought about that, Dan. But it can't happen, we can't get caught, any of us. Whether the mission fails or succeeds, no one will ever know it took place. President Rump will be the last person to talk about it or to want it to become public, believe me. It's fail safe in that respect. And, when one day it does become known, which is inevitable, I suppose, no one will believe it. It'll just be another conspiracy theory propagated and shared by suckers, cranks and losers."

"Anyone for a *digestif*?" asked Schurz. They both concurred.

"It'll have to be one for the road, I'm afraid," said O'Reilly. "I've an early meeting with my DGSE counterpart; the chief of Internal Security will be there too. Two questions about your fairy tale, Stephen: Why are you sharing your plot with me? Secondly, do you even begin to imagine how many people would have to be in on the secret aside from Rump's G7 colleagues? On the face of it, dozens if not hundreds, you know."

"Well, Sir, Dan … I confess that the original idea was to go through the foreign ministers, since we potentially had Ormrod on our side from the start. Then we ran straight into the problem of Secretary Holden before we even considered approaching any of the others. From what we know of him, we wouldn't have had a chance."

"You're right there, no discussion."

"So, my wife suggested liaising rather with the chiefs of the G7 foreign intelligence agencies and, well, your name came into the picture and here we are."

O'Reilly laughed gaily.

"So, it's a *family* affair, your project to save us all from a nuclear apocalypse!"

He's mocking me, thought Blakely, he doesn't believe a word of all I've told him.

"As for the large number of people who have to be involved, you know about that question better than me, Dan. After all, it's uniquely a question of security, of the army I'm told surrounds your President. They're the only people I'm really worried about. On the other hand, all we need is a little inattention here and there and a handful of good people on our side. For the others, our double *will* be Rump – they simply won't know the difference."

"Very interesting." That's all O'Reilly said.

"And now I'm off. I'll catch a taxi on the boulevard, don't worry about me. It was a really fun evening, thanks to both you young men. I'll give you a call tomorrow, Scott, we must do this again before I go back to the States. And I'll take those pictures, if you don't mind, son," he said, pointing to the collection on the table.

They sat in silence. Blakely had one ear cocked for the screech of tires, the shout of orders, the crash of the bar door against its hinges. He looked nervously at the entrance for the arrival of the burly hoodlums who would scatter the ta-

bles, yank him from his seat, drag him out of the Rosebud
and throw him into the car, destination Cuba.

CHAPTER 19

THE SPYMASTERS MEET

General Gianfranco Geppetto arrived late and last at the meeting. This was nothing unusual. Only when Greeks and Spaniards were attending did he have anything close to rivalry for his tardiness.

Geppetto, a devout man, had been obliged to pray a little longer than usual that morning. He believed in ridding himself of guilt well before it had a chance to build an appetite and eat at the table of his conscience. Yes, he confessed to the embassy chaplain, he had ceded to the advances of a *mademoiselle* of debatable morals the previous night and been *infedele* to Signora Geppetto; but Paris was, after all, Paris and the ladies extremely difficult to resist.

Father Ancelotti, who had no weakness at all for women, had muttered something about the folly of such behavior for the head of Italian foreign security, and largely left it at that. A few more supplications to the patron saint of his agency, quite unaccountably an Englishman, Sir Thomas More, and he walked back out into the lovely Parisian spring morning a free man again.

Geppetto wore a black patch over his left eye. For this, he was known among his troops as *Il Pirata*, a sobriquet of which he was very fond. No one except Mrs. Geppetto knew what the patch concealed, if anything.

"Ah, *buongiorno, caro Generale!*" said Gilles Haubois, the host, as Geppetto saluted each of his colleagues, individually, with a shower of excuses for making them wait for him. No one in the world can apologize as beautifully and compellingly as an Italian, mused Haubois.

"Now, my friends, we can begin," said the head of the French external services. He had already asked all the other officials, aides de camp and secretaries, to leave the room. There were only eight of them now: the aforementioned General Geppetto, Marshal Tuoma Nakajima, Sir Harry Peterson, Haubois, Robert Pensec, O'Reilly, Vincent Collins and Major General Hans Hopfinger, known to the others and greatly to his irritation, as 'Goldfinger'.

"I welcome you with great pleasure to Paris, also on behalf of my colleague from the interior services, Robert Pensec. I do hope that you don't mind, but we have changed the order of today's agenda to bring forward our discussion on Bangistan. This is why I have asked your staff to leave; what you are about to hear is highly confidential."

Only the German, Hopfinger, raised his eyebrows at this quintessentially offhand French behavior. They had spent weeks exchanging messages about the agenda, fixing the order of each point, only for everything to be changed again on the day. "*Typisch*," he muttered a little more loudly than he intended.

"Yes, I'm sorry, Major General, but we wouldn't have done so if new elements had not arisen, matters that demand our most urgent attention. When you hear what we have to say, you will fully understand."

Two others in the room knew already what he meant. O'Reilly, of course, who had arranged it all, and Sir Harry, who had been briefed the previous day by Ormrod, in a long call, and then in person by the First Secretary at the embassy. That left only the German, the Japanese, the Canadian and the Italian temporarily in the dark.

In an adjacent room sat Scott Schurz and Stephen Blakely. They were both struggling to stay awake, having been up all the night preparing their script.

"Can you believe we're here, that we've come this far?" asked Blakely.

"I'm stunned," said Schurz. "I can only put it down to your indestructible conviction that this mad scheme could actually work. I really wonder if anything so insane has ever been tried. But one after another, you've won people over to it."

"Yes, one after the other," said Blakely vacantly.

They both yawned, then laughed.

It was O'Reilly who came to bring them in.

"How's the mood?" Schurz asked him.

"Difficult to say. These are very unusual people, you know. All I can say is that they are all very fond of intrigue. That's how they got in to this business in the first place. So, make it very *intriguing*, if you would."

After introductions and the presentation of the meeting participants, Blakely was given the floor as Schurz set up his computer to show slides.

"With your permission, Sir," he said turning to Haubois, "I would, with respect, like to impress on you all the extremely secret nature of the project I am about to describe."

"I should say we're the right guys for secrets, wouldn't you, Blakely?" said Collins, the Canadian, to general amusement.

"Haha. Yes, indeed, indeed. I would also like to say that what I and my colleague Scott Schurz are going to propose is completely *unofficial* and not known to our respective governments; it has not been approved by either of them – yet, at least.

"In fact, our opinion is that it should stay that way. If, by any chance, you approve the plan, you will be asked, each of you, to tell only *one* other person."

"And who might that be?" enquired Hopfinger.

"In your case, Sir, the Chancellor."

"It's that important, then?" remarked the German.

"It's both of vital importance and, how can I put it … extremely *unorthodox*," said Blakely. "We simply cannot go through the usual channels and involve other politicians or officials. This is why we have come directly to you. Everything hangs on your actions and engagement. Without you, there is no plan. Might I ask if each of you *does* have direct, private access to your leaders, before I start?"

The spymasters all nodded their confirmation silently.

"Very good," said Blakely. "Let me show you a couple of photographs."

The first slides they put up were full-length, Hawkins portraits of Marie-Pierre Etxeberria wearing a dress. Everyone laughed.

"So it's blackmail, is it?" asked Hopfinger. "Rump signs for peace or this goes viral?"

"Come, come, nothing quite so crude," said O'Reilly, smiling. "Go on, Stephen."

Blakely first reminded them of the context. At present, they were all the idle, impotent spectators of an impending catastrophe. Nothing anybody could say or do could divert the runaway train of mere chance from its course. Global security lay in the hands and head of a single man who listened to no advice, who acted out of instinct alone and had proven to be highly unpredictable. If President Rump botched the talks in Petrobangorski, there would be no second occasion to salvage peace from the jaws of conflict, he concluded gravely.

"No more Hiroshima! No more Nagasaki!" said a trembling Marshal Nakajima with emotion, bowing slightly in his seat.

"Hear, hear," the others concurred in unison.

"Of all this, we are perfectly aware, Blakely," said Collins after allowing the moment of collective emotion to pass. "But I think that I speak also for my colleagues if I insist that you get to the point. What's the plan? That's what we all want to know."

"The point, gentlemen, is that I don't think that our nations can allow any of this to happen. Extraordinary circumstances demand extraordinary actions. We believe that, with your cooperation, we can stop Rump from ever getting to Bangistan; that we can replace him *en route* with a double – you have just seen her – and that, in the absence of the real President, we can control the discussions and perhaps reach an agreement that ensures the denuclearization of the Akim regime and enduring peace."

They all stared at him without a word. Then Hopfinger reacted.

"This is impossible."

"*Impossible* is precisely our business," said Geppetto cheerfully. "There is only one thing that we do better than the impossible – and that is the *improbable*! This is our art. So far, I like what I hear. It is very improbable indeed! Go on, young man."

"Share some of the detail, Stephen, if you will," added Sir Harry, who was anxious to hear the story a second time, after his unbelievable first briefing the previous day.

Blakely obliged once more. The zucchini woman, the switch in Versailles, the rôle of Rump's G7 colleagues, the second airplane, the pitch in Petrobangorski, the second switch two days later in Paris, the news conference and, most importantly, the reasons why the American President would stay silent about the whole affair, whether it succeeded or in the unlikely event that the mission failed.

"You will see that none of your leaders will be taking any risks at all. I know that will be your major concern. On the contrary, they will be able to boast that it was they who helped avert war by their persuasiveness with Rump in the Versailles talks. Everyone will win. Really, everyone."

"Security," said Marshal Nakajima, without elaboration.

"Maybe I could come in here," said O'Reilly. "You are right Marshal, that's of course the major challenge. As you are all aware, it's our Secret Service that takes care of the President's personal protection, not the CIA. And they really don't give him an inch to move; they'll be crawling all over the place on the whole trip. Two things, though. The Director is an excellent, close friend of mine and his political sympathies are, what should I say, not exactly *compatible* with the current White House, to put it mildly. I don't think it's beyond the realm of imagination that he and a few of his most loyal people might turn their heads in the wrong direction at the right moment. Secondly, I don't suppose that Secret Service agents have been especially trained to spot doppelgängers. My belief is that they won't even notice, or if they do, will rather question their own sanity than the reality. I've already had a few words with the Director and we've fixed to meet as soon as I get back to Washington."

"And our French friends?" asked Geppetto. "All this is supposed to take place on your territory. Can you possibly go along with it? Take the risk of destroying the trust of your American friends for another hundred years?"

"We don't trust each other *that* much even now, do we Dan?" laughed Haubois. "We have, of course, discussed all this prior to this meeting, together with Robert and our young diplomats here. In short, we think that though indeed *improbable*, the plan is not impossible. Of course, there are a thousand dispositions to be taken, details to be resolved, but we have five weeks to deal with them and can stop or go forward at any time."

"And your President?" asked Hopfinger. "Do you think he'll agree to this mad adventure?"

"We think so, yes. He loves *innovation*, doing things differently from the others, from what has ever before even been conceived. I am sure that not only will he be very excited about the plan, but he will see its merits as an act of *retribution*, something we French are very keen on. After all, Rump has already screwed up his climate ambitions, his plans for Iran, his dreams for European integration, and much else. It will be a very sweet little revenge. And, Major General, if you need a little help with your Chancellor, I am sure that the President would be only too happy to oblige. They get on very well, as you know."

"What are the blind spots, the strengths and weaknesses of the plan, the threats and opportunities?" asked Collins, addressing his question to both Blakely and Schurz. He was a graduate of a top Toronto management school and thus could perhaps be forgiven his stupid question.

"I see two challenges for the moment," said the American. "Persuading this French peasant woman to take a trip to Bangistan and, once in Petrobangorski, concealing the fact that she doesn't speak a word of English and, indeed, believes that she is there to sell zucchini. We haven't yet come up with the solutions, but we'll manage. We have a man on the spot, our Ambassador, who will be brought into the picture in good time and who can help us on those matters."

"Fortunately," Blakely took over, "Hakim Akim doesn't speak a word of English either, which eliminates at least one piece of the linguistic conundrum. The other problem is how to pull the wool over the eyes of Akim's interpreters, but we'll surely come up with an idea. Monsieur Pensec, do you by any chance have anyone in your services who speaks Gascon?"

"Gascon? No problem," said Pensec. "Leave it to me. In my services, we have Gascon agents, Basque agents, Occitan agents, Breton agents, Catalans, Corsicans, even Savoyans. We are a very fractious people, you know, the French. So we keep a close eye on everybody. You never know when the ugly head of regional independence will suddenly show itself!"

They discussed various other details and potential obstacles and saw rapidly that a lot of work had to be done before the plan could really be confirmed. Haubois summed up the situation, then asked for their consent to move forward with the first steps.

"Are you in agreement that this unusual project is worth further exploration and our best endeavors to succeed with it? Maybe we need to hear a word of conclusion from the man who has most to lose."

They all looked at Dan O'Reilly.

"It's your President," said Collins. "You know how much we hold him in our hearts."

They all laughed.

"I think we should try it," said O'Reilly. "A war with Bangistan could cause the most terrible damage and strife for all of us. It is our moral duty to endeavor to avoid that conflict at all costs. It seems to me that our young friends have stumbled across a way to do it."

They didn't even vote on it. In their hearts, even the most timid and least introspective of them, they knew that if there were actually any purpose at all in their lives, on this occasion they had a moral obligation to act for the general good. Before they concluded on this agenda point, only Geppetto spoke.

"We need, of course, a name for this operation!"

Everyone grunted his agreement and began to cogitate.

The first to speak up was Marshal Nakajima.

"*Kagemusha*. Operation Kagemusha."

There was a respectful silence. No one appeared to catch the meaning. Then Pensec spoke.

"Brilliant, *mon Maréchal*! Absolutely *géniale*!"

"What does *that* signify?" asked the skeptical Hopfinger.

"You haven't seen the Kurosawa movie?" said Pensec. "The idiot who replaces the dying warlord, to dissuade his enemies from taking advantage of the situation and attacking? The double?"

"You're right," said O'Reilly. "Of course. Marshal, that is a wonderful inspiration! What does it mean, though, if anything?"

"Decoy," said Nakajima simply. "Political decoy."

It was settled on the instant. Operation Kagemusha was born.

CHAPTER 20

THE TRACTOR IS BLESSED, THE MISSION IS ON

Freshly appointed as commercial director, Adela Laperye was the newest member of staff of the Blakely-Schurz Fruit & Vegetable Export Company. In fact, she was the only employee. A part-time hairdresser in Pau, she was also an occasional agent of the French interior intelligence services. She owed this singular position chiefly to the fact that, in addition to French, English, Spanish and Basque, she spoke eight dialects of Occitan, including the three varieties of Gascon, one of them a Pyrenean language of whistles.

"And our client, I assume she speaks the Béarnese dialect?" Adela asked her new bosses.

Blakely and Schurz looked at each other and laughed.

"Really sorry," said Blakely, "but we have no idea. Is it important?"

"Not at all. I was just curious."

Adela had come up to Paris to be briefed on her mission. She would be going all the way to Petrobangorski with them, so they held back nothing of the plot. Pensec had assured them that she was a rock, one of his finest, and they trusted him. She listened carefully, patiently and without interruption, as the two young men spoke in turn of Luchère-Les-Bains, the zucchini, the poor and suspicious Etxeberrias, Martin Guerre and Shi Pei Pu, the farm equipment, the spare, uncultivated field, the influence and avarice of the Mayor – a potential ally – the farmers' ignorance of the world at large, the fact that Bangistan might as well be on the moon as far as they were concerned, the initial antagonism of Marie-Pierre to them and to their export plan, the complexities of the switch and the meeting with Akim.

"So," said Blakely, "you are not walking into a *fait accompli*, by any means. We have led the horse to the water, but you must make it drink. With all respect to Madame Etxeberria, of course."

Adela looked at the men and exclaimed happily: "*Quelle histoire*! What a story! To summarize: I have to convince her to leave her farm, to come to Paris, and to fly half-way to Asia dressed like a man. And you will '*take care of the rest*'."

"Yeah, that about sums up your mission," said Schurz, smiling. "We're really trying to take this step by step, detail by detail, you know. There are numerous questions we haven't yet resolved. At any moment, the whole thing could be called off. Right now, absolutely everything hangs on you, on your ability to persuade Marie-Pierre Etxeberria to go to Petrobangorski to sign this export contract. Without which, I hasten to add, there will be no deal and no more aid for the development of her farm."

"I confess that I had never heard of this place, this country Bangistan, until a few weeks ago," said Adela.

"Believe me, you were certainly not alone, not by any means," said Blakely. "We're diplomats, we're supposed to know these things for a living, and frankly we didn't. The Americans even had an *ambassador* there and were practically unaware of it. You'll meet him, a certain Winkelmeier. He'll come in very useful to get on-the-ground information as we move forward."

"What about our phantom business, the Blakely-Schurz enterprise? What have you told them about that? What do I need to know?"

"We said nothing at all and they asked nothing," said Blakely. "So you can just make it all up. But make sure that you remember what you said, so we don't contradict you further on down the road."

"So, when can you go to Luchère, Adela?" asked Schurz.

"I fly back to Pau tonight and can drive over to the farm tomorrow, if you can fix it up. Just give me a call and let me know."

"And what are you doing for the rest of the day until your flight?"

"Shopping. I don't get up to Paris very much, you know. And almost never for work like this."

Adela declined to join them for lunch and off she went alone to the Faubourg Saint-Honoré.

*

Blakely located Lizarazu at Chez Irène and asked if he could arrange for a message to be given to the Etxeberrias and for someone to await a response. There was no telephone at the farm.

"We're sending down our commercial director, Adela Laperye, to discuss the details of the export contract and the signing procedures. We're lucky. She speaks Gascon fluently."

The Mayor rang back two hours later to say that all had been fixed. The Etxeberrias would expect Mademoiselle Laperye tomorrow around mid-day when they broke from their labors for lunch.

*

As she waded through the mud into the courtyard of the Etxeberria farm, Adela crossed the path of a departing priest.

"You're late for the *fête*," said the Father, clutching his skirts up around his naked, bony thighs. "The tractor is already blessed."

Adela smiled and wished him a good day. She didn't know what he was talking about, but she had been well trained in this respect. Never spontaneously admit that you don't understand what someone is telling you, that is what she had been taught. Those who learn the most are those who ask 'why' the least, according to intelligence agency psychologists. She had found that this was more often than not quite true. People had a terrible compulsion to talk if only one would let them. In any case, it was a good path to follow within the independentist milieux that she had infiltrated. They indeed did not like people who asked questions. It shut them up very quickly.

Rounding the barn wall, she encountered a dozen or more people drinking and laughing in front of a glistening, bright red tractor. She spotted Ronald Rump instantly. *Incroyable*, she said to herself, *tout simplement incroyable*. She was not supposed to know what Madame Etxeberria looked like, so enquired of the first person she met. By chance, it was Gaston.

"You are Mademoiselle Adela, perhaps?" he asked her in Basque, which she understood just as well as all the other languages of the region. "Have a drink, please. We are celebrating the arrival of our new tractor, as you see. Isn't it beautiful? We are very happy so far with your enterprise," he laughed.

She laughed too, and added: "I am pleased also. It is indeed a very fine tractor."

Adela took the plastic cup that Gaston gave her and symbolically toasted the tractor with the other guests, neighboring farmers, who had turned to the newcomer. Introductions were made, while some of the others suggested slyly that she might have a need also for cabbages, or potatoes, or turnips for export and, if so, was most welcome to come and see their products too. Finally, she stood shaking the firm hand of

Marie-Pierre Etxeberria, who towered more than a foot above her. They liked each other instantly. It was rare, she told Adela, to find a young woman who spoke Gascon so well these days. Confidence was established. The guile and charisma of Mademoiselle Lapeyre did the rest.

*

That evening, Adela called Schurz to report. He called Blakely the moment after.

"Why did she call you, not me?" asked Blakely.

"My superior charm, I guess. Actually, we've fallen in love. She doesn't know it yet, but women are slow about those things."

"Are you nuts? The three of us only met for two hours."

"Be that as it may, Stephen, she's going to be the mother of my children. But I've got to hang up now to think about it," said Schurz.

"Wait, wait. You haven't even told me what she said, Romeo, you idiot."

"Against my love, it is as nothing," Schurz said gravely. Before shouting in to his mobile: "We're on! My sweetheart did it! Marie-Pierre agreed to go to Bangistan! Operation Kagemusha moves forward!"

"Good Lord," said Blakely. "That's fantastic. I really wonder how your Adela did it."

"Oh, it was quite simple, apparently. She promised that the company – i.e. the British Embassy – would buy the refrigerated storehouse."

"Jesus. How am I going to get *that* through. When are you Americans going to chip in some money, anyhow?"

"We can't, you know, without provoking suspicion. O'Reilly says he cannot possibly pass such things off on the CIA budget. So, for the moment, you're our bank, *old chap*."

"But tell me more, Scott, I want to hear everything, every word she told you."

"Well, it seems they hit it off like a house on fire – Adela is already '*ma petite*', the little one. Marie-Pierre was at first very reluctant indeed to travel, but when she heard that her personal presence was needed at the contract signing, that it was a *legal obligation*, she couldn't find an argument against it. The promise of a modern coldstore tipped the balance, apparently. Also the chance to get away from Gaston and his stinking sheep for a few days, she told Adela."

Blakely laughed. He could barely believe their good fortune.

"Did your Adela also bring up the dress question?"

"It fell into her lap like a ripened fruit, Stephen. Marie-Pierre said she couldn't possibly meet a President wearing the rags in her wardrobe. Adela not only promised her new clothes for the trip, but explained that they would have to be very *masculine*, because of the religious mania of the Bangistani about how women appear in public. So Adela and I have agreed to go shopping together in a week or so for the typical garments of a six foot three man. Adela actually thinks Marie-Pierre is taller than Rump, but a couple of inches don't matter in the slightest, of course."

"I thought you hated shopping, Scott."

"Love sweeps away all such trivial antipathies," said Schurz. "But now I really to have to run. I've also got a day-time job, you know."

And with that he cut off the call.

"Our Lady of Lourdes, I take back all I said," Blakely joked to himself. "Stay with me a little longer, won't you?"

The Blessed Virgin Mary, for her own best reasons, remained at Stephen Blakely's side. Everything fell into place, without a single hitch.

One by one, the spy chiefs reported back to O'Reilly.

"Dann mal los!"

"On y va!"

"Ikimashou!"

"Andiamo, miei cari - my darlings!"

"Let's go!"

All the G7 leaders, minus one, of course, had given their assent.

This was all that O'Reilly needed to set the Kagemusha machine in full motion.

CHAPTER 21

NIGHT AT THE CHATEAU

They all gathered in Angela's room after the lights had been turned off in the Chateau. Each made his way to Marie-Antoinette's main apartment, conceded to the Chancellor as the senior of the female guests. They crept along the corridors by the light of the torches provided for them by their hosts. Heads of State or not, they still needed to use the bathroom, and these were outside the royal suites. Emmanuel brought the rope.

The morning's 'Mr. President', 'Madam Chancellor', 'Mr.' or 'Mrs. Prime Minister', had given way to familiarity and first names again, as was custom when all the officials were out of the picture and they were left alone.

The G7 agenda that day had been unproblematic. How could anyone be against *gender equality, peace, fighting poverty*? Fine, Rump had taken a walk while they were discussing climate change, but they expected nothing else from him. So full was he of the upcoming peace talks in Bangistan, he would sign any damn declaration of intent they put in front of him and indeed he did so without reading it. Promises only commit those who believe them. This was the President's political philosophy.

Angela, Emmanuel, Justin, Shinzo and Giuseppe were waiting for Theresa, the last to arrive. In the meantime, they helped themselves to drinks from Marie-Antoinette's well-stocked bar. Finally, a quiet knock was heard on the suite door and the Prime Minister walked in.

"This isn't a pyjama party, Theresa!" Emmanuel exclaimed, to general amusement.

Theresa looked down at her bathrobe and around the room at her fully-clothed colleagues and said, crossly: "Well, no one told *me* we had to get dressed!"

Only a very large gin and tonic served in a golden chalice, which Giuseppe galantly offered her without being asked, placated the Prime Minister and brought back her calm and her timid smile. They then got down to serious discussions.

As usual, and without invitation, Emmanuel took charge and control. It was a persistent, irritating bad habit of his.

"You all know the plan," said the President. "But I have a new idea. If we screw up tomorrow, for whatever reason, Kagemusha is doomed to failure, with all that this implies. I think, therefore, we must have a Plan B. Unusually, perhaps, it is a Plan B we would have to try before the Plan A. But as Hegel said …"

"Fuck Hegel!" came a proposal from the settee. Shinzo was a man of few, but powerful, words in English and when he was drunk, as now, he liked to deploy them. "I just want bed."

"Right," said Emmanuel, "I'll make it short. You have all had detailed notes for tomorrow. I hope that you've memorized and destroyed them. You all know your rôles. There is only one variable, one thing that could affect the outcome: That the weather is shit and Rump refuses to go for a walk. But the forecast is good, bright sun and not a cloud. Anyone have any doubts about what they have to do?"

"When will you give me the duct tape?" asked Giuseppe.

"You might as well have it now." Emmanuel reached into his pocket, pulled out the roll of tape and lobbed it to him.

"I have one question too," said Angela. "Why is it *me* who has to kneel down in the mud?"

"Well, *chère* Angela, you are, what can we say, the most

... the most ... *robust* among us! This is a compliment, you know."

No, thought Angela, it is not a compliment at all, young man.

"Any questions, Justin?" asked Emmanuel.

As the President had suspected, Justin was still torturing himself about the morality of the whole plan. He'll be useless on the day, thought Emmanuel, who had assigned him the completely futile role of 'lookout'.

"No," said Justin.

They ran over the details quickly. Emmanuel suggested that they cut the rope right there and then, to have it in readiness in the morning. He brought out his pocket knife and measuring carefully, while Giuseppe and Justin held the ends, he sliced it unequally into a dozen pieces - a couple for each of them to carry hidden on them on the walk, lest Rump get suspicious.

As Emmanuel worried about the lengths of the pieces, Justin said helpfully that he had learnt to tie knots very well in the boy scouts and that he could certainly put them together again tomorrow if it proved necessary.

Shinzo, who had now put his feet up and was settling in for the night, nevertheless asked: "And Plan B?"

"Thanks, Shinzo," said Emmanuel. "It's this: we actually do the job *now* and keep him in the Chateau instead of the garden. I have a room ready, but it's much more dangerous, since there are many, many guards and staff around in the daytime and someone might stumble across him. But we should try anyhow, because it eliminates the variable."

They all nodded.

"Theresa, how special is your *special relationship*?" asked Emmanuel, turning to the Prime Minister and winking.

"I don't know what you mean," the Prime Minister replied a little snootily.

"No, no, I wasn't implying anything at all, Theresa, I expressed myself badly. I mean would it seem very strange if you knocked on his door right now and asked for a chat?"

"Yes, I suppose it would. Heads of State we may be, but we are nevertheless humans and don't go around knocking on each other's bedroom doors at midnight. He could get the wrong idea, you know his reputation. What if he misunderstands, takes a fancy to me? Grabs me!"

"*Altamente improbabile,*" muttered Giuseppe, drawing a look from Theresa that could have killed *fifty* Italian Prime Ministers.

"What do you have in mind, anyhow, if I agree to do it?"

"Maybe just talk to him for a while, check out his room, see if there are any agents under his bed, judge whether it would be feasible for us to come in and jump him right now. Maybe it's a crazy idea, but I'd like you to get a sense of our options and to report back."

"Zo, I get to kneel down in the mud, and Theresa gets to play … to play … *Mata Hari*!" said Angela resentfully.

In truth, though, the Chancellor could forgive Emmanuel anything. Those beautiful clear-blue eyes; the tender way he held her hand and caressed it with his thumb; that kiss on her forehead in Compiègne! *Sehr, sehr schön.* Joachim had been jealous and had created quite a scene when she returned home to Berlin.

Theresa thought the whole idea was stupid and too risky, but agreed anyhow to go through with it. She snatched a few pieces of rope from Emmanuel, stuffed them in her bathrobe and marched off haughtily on her mission. If they didn't hear from her within thirty minutes, Plan B had failed, as she fully expected, and she was off to get a good night's sleep. She would see them again at 7 a.m. in front of Angela's suite. In the unlikely event that the plan worked, she would alert Emmanuel and he could take it from there, make further arrangements and let the others know.

Angela kicked Shinzo off Marie-Antoinette's sofa and pushed them all out of her room.

*

Ronald Rump was lying in Louis 14th's bed watching Fox News and eating the best cheeseburger of his life, made for him personally by the *grand chef* of the Chateau's restaurant, Alain Ducasse, who had earlier in the evening watched miserably as the President hid his pheasant fricasée in a pot of potato purée after pushing aside with disdain his pumpkin *consommé*. But Monsieur Ducasse held no grudges; he was there simply to please.

Rump was guffawing between bites. "Hannity can't pronounce 'Petrobangorski' either," he chuckled. "That's the fifth time he's screwed it up!"

There was a knock. "It's Theresa," said the Prime Minister, seeing that the light was on and hearing the television and pushing the door slightly open.

"Come on in, Theresa. There's a Fox News special on my Bangistan trip. Come and watch it if you like."

"That's kind of you, Mr. President, dear Ronald, but I have another proposal for you."

At that moment, a piece of rope fell out of the Prime Minister's bathrobe pocket on the floor by Rump's bedside. She stared at it in horror.

"Now, Theresa, I know how much you like me and I enjoyed holding hands with you in the Rose Garden, and you do look very nice in your negligé, I'm sure, but it really isn't the moment. I'm not into that stuff anyhow, despite what the Fake News says."

They both laughed gaily.

"I was just kidding, of course, Ronald! I really wanted to remind you of our walk in the morning before you go. You promised to join us all, do you remember? We want to wish you good luck and send our blessings with you on your trip to Bangistan. It'll have to be early, though, we're told your schedule is very tight."

Rump confirmed that he'd be happy to walk in the gardens with them before taking off. Theresa and the others would pick him up just after seven o'clock, she promised.

"If it isn't raining, of course," added Rump. "If that's the case, just leave me to catch another hour of sleep."

The President did wonder why on earth the Prime Minister was wandering around the Chateau at night carrying a rope, but then the British were peculiar like that, he thought. Perhaps it's only to keep her pyjama bottoms up, he speculated.

CHAPTER 22

THE ABDUCTION

Angela, Giuseppe, Shinzo, Emmanuel, Theresa and Justin jumped out of their beds at the crack of dawn, rushed to their windows and threw aside the heavy curtains. The sun was shining. The sky was blue. Operation Kagemusha was *on*.

They all dressed hastily, drank the tea or coffee that had been left outside their rooms by Chateau staff, and proceeded to the meeting point outside Angela's rooms. They then made their way in a group to Louis 14th's chambers. The few security agents who were about at that time were either Pensec's or O'Reilly's men. Rump was waiting for them, his bags packed and ready for pick up.

"Don't worry about them," Emmanuel told him, pointing to the suitcases. "You'll find them again in the helicopter. Now come and see our beautiful gardens and tell us once more your plans for peace with Bangistan."

The Estate of the Palace of Versailles covers two thousand acres in a vast medley of gardens, lawns, canals, basins, fountains, pavilions and groves. The woodlands are so extensive that a man could get lost in them for days …

Several golf carts awaited them with dependable agents at their wheels. O'Reilly, together with the Director of the Secret Service, Haubois, and Pensec, had done their work well. The French President invited his American colleague to drive one of the carts if he wished to. "These vehicles are very familiar to you, I think," he told him.

Rump, with the Frenchman giving directions at his side, drove off down the Royal Way, the three other carts close behind them. Just before Apollo's Fountain, Emmanuel indicated a turn to the left, towards the groves, where he called for a halt and invited everyone to walk a little among the verdant galleries, leafy palisades and chestnut trees.

"Can you imagine, Ronald, you'll be in Petrobangorski for lunch?" said Justin to strike up a conversation.

"Does seem kinda odd," said Rump, "but I'm ready for it. My advisors told me not to go, you know, but a man's gotta do what a man's gotta do. Peace depends on it. And, if I don't come away with peace, I'm just going to have to show those sons-of-bitches that they made a really bad mistake to think they could fool around with America."

As they entered the enclosed Colonnade Grove and ambled around the circular arcade between marble pilasters and columns, Emmanuel signalled to Justin with his eyes to stay back at the entrance on the lookout. Giuseppe had walked on ahead a little and identified the point where a section of the latticed palisade had been removed.

Angela was trembling with anxiety and could barely walk; Shinzo was uncharacteristically and incomprehensibly talking his very head off, though no one paid attention to him; Giuseppe lingered in front of the missing fence, boasting noisily about the Tuscan marble that surrounded them; Emmanuel was recounting to an amused Rump some of the more salacious tales of royal goings-on in the Versailles groves. Only Theresa looked completely passive and unmoved, as though she hadn't anything at all to do with the imminent actions and was mentally elsewhere.

Emmanuel, who held Rump's arm, stopped them both by Giuseppe's side, and turned the American gently towards the center of the grove where a group sculpture depicted Pluto abducting Proserpine. He was still talking about the majestic nocturnal orgies that had taken place in the Versailles gardens during the reign of Louis 15th and leant even closer to the President to whisper a particularly scabrous detail …

Right on cue, Angela slumped to her hands and knees a few inches behind Rump on the grassy border of the arcade. Emmanuel, who was now gripping the American fondly by both arms, freed his hands and thrust them violently against the President's shoulders. Shinzo and Theresa, who had also slipped up behind Rump, caught his arms in the fall. Pushing the kneeling Angela unceremoniously out of his way, Giuseppe sat on the stunned American's chest, whipped out his duct tape and stuck it across his mouth, from ear to ear. Shinzo and Emmanuel had now pulled his fists together and tied them with a section of rope. Though Rump lashed out with both legs, he could do nothing against the three men and his feet too were soon subjugated and trussed.

Together, they dragged the President a hundred yards or so into the surrounding thicket and left him there, leaning against a chestnut, one more rope tied around the tree and his waist to make sure he couldn't move at all. Emmanuel dispatched a prepared text message from his phone and they walked off slowly back to the grove and then out to the golf cars. Others would take over now. They had done their job and done it well, like real pros.

Justin was the only one to speak. He had seen nothing from his post as lookout.

"And so? Did everything go according to plan?" he asked anxiously.

Two or three of them nodded. They all felt troubled and confused and not especially proud of themselves either. The dreadful look of panic and fear in Rump's eyes had gotten to all of them. None of them liked the President, but that changed nothing. Terror on a man's face is not a pretty sight. But, after all, world peace was at stake, they each told themselves in their own way.

The group drove off in procession further away still from the Chateau, beyond the gardens and into the woods and fields of the Park. They circumvented the Grand Canal and stopped only when they were near the outer perimeter, within view of a helicopter whose rotors were already turning slowly. They were almost two miles away from the Chateau and out of sight of onlookers, but nevertheless went through the motions of farewell, even blowing kisses to the pilots. Soon the helicopter rose gently into the air and slid off back over the Versailles Estate, passing by the Chateau where hundreds of G7 officials had gathered to shout 'good luck' into the skies and wave at the President's five departing suitcases.

*

Another crowd waited for the helicopter at Orly Airport, where Air Force One sat in a remote area of the airfield. It never arrived. But here too, O'Reilly and his men had taken care of everything. His friend the Secret Service Director gathered his agents and the President's guests who were waiting to board, and explained that, unhappily, the plane had technical problems and that they would not be flying that day. President Rump was going to Bangistan by other means. It was not their custom or right to ask questions about these confidential matters and they all resigned themselves to discovering the pleasures of Petrobangorski some other time.

Twenty miles away, at a French military airbase, O'Reilly, Ormrod, Blakely, Schurz, Marie-Pierre Etxeberria, Adela Laperye, and three CIA agents, boarded an unmarked Gulfstream business jet occasionally used to transport US Presidents on delicate foreign visits. Champagne was served within minutes.

Just before take-off, O'Reilly cabled Winkelmeier.

"Very small delegation. Obliged to switch aircraft after

technical problems. Just ten of us. Plan accordingly, cancel all but one floor of rooms below Presidential suites. Important: Rump not Rump. Under no circumstances show surprise when she speaks Gascon. Operation Kagemusha is underway. All will be explained."

For the next forty-eight hours, Dan O'Reilly, Director of the CIA, and George Ormrod, the United Kingdom Foreign Minister, were Co-Chairmen of the Blakely-Schurz Fruit & Vegetable Export Company. But only, of course, in the eyes of Marie-Pierre Etxeberria, who was impressed to have them along on the trip after Adela explained their positions in the enterprise.

A glass of champagne in her hand, staring out of the plane window as they rose above the clouds, she thought to herself: "Goodness me, what a lark. I feel like a President!" She had only one regret and that was the confiscation of her suitcase of zucchini at the airport. Adela had explained the strict measures currently in force at Bangistan borders to prohibit the entrance of fresh products, for fear of plant pests or animal diseases. They would have to make do with the photographs brought along by Monsieur Blakely and, in any case, Hakim Akim had already had the pleasure of tasting her produce. It all seemed reasonable to Marie-Pierre. There was only one thing gnawing away at her mind – at what price per kilo or ton should she start the negotiations? No one had even spoken of this yet, much to her surprise.

In Petrobangorski, Winkelmeier had received O'Reilly's cable before leaving for Akim Airport. The world is completely off its hinges, he said to himself.

CHAPTER 23

ARRIVAL IN PETROBANGORSKI

The band on the runway was practising what Winkelmeier guessed might possibly be construed, with a generous effort of the imagination, as The Star-Spangled Banner.

He was alone with the musicians. No other official presence at all could yet be seen on behalf of the Bangistani authorities. There was a rumor, but nothing more than that, that Akim might after all come personally to greet Rump. That would be usual, of course, but nothing was quite what it should be in Petrobangorski. They had no experience whatsoever of State visits by anyone at all, let alone a US President.

Winkelmeier had done what he could, guided by the instructions he had received from O'Reilly a week earlier. Many of the CIA chief's injunctions were in direct contradiction with the more formal demands made by his boss, Holden. But since the first was coming to Bangistan with the President, and the other was staying in Washington, it was not difficult to choose whose orders to follow. On one matter, he had no choice to make. They had both insisted that Yogi Akim should be kept well away from the negotiations; O'Reilly, because he knew that Akim spoke English and was, if not a man of the world, at least a little travelled and therefore a risk; Holden, because he wanted vengeance for his own exclusion and because he feared Yogi Akim might outsmart Rump, which was not the greatest challenge a man could face, after all. The Great Leader had his own reason for getting his brother out of the picture. He did not want him to know the price at which he was selling peace, to avoid any squabbling about its division at a later date. Yogi Akim, with barely a protest, was dispatched to Zurich to complete his previous mission. He was out of the way and everyone was happy about it.

Half the planet's media wanted to cover the summit. There was a broad consensus on this matter too. It was agreed that they should be kept well away, thrown off planes heading for Petrobangorski and stopped at all border crossings from Russia and China. If any reporters made it through the blockade, orders had been given to arrest them on sight. Only Rump really desired their presence and made a fuss about it; if he was making history, he wanted it live on Fox. Akim, on the other hand, was happy not to have journalists crawling all over his country, poking their noses into his business. He insisted only that Bangistani state television should record a handful of summit highlights; he promised that they would share them for foreign distribution with international news agencies and syndicates. For a modest 'technical fee', of course.

O'Reilly's orders to Winkelmeier had been rather enigmatic and conspiratorial, as befitted his functions. But they had not included the latest perplexing information. The Ambassador looked once more at the cable. "Rump is not Rump". What did that mean? He was out of sorts? Not really himself? Unhappy? Unwell? It didn't matter how long he stared at the paper, he didn't guess its meaning. "He" was in fact "she"? The President would speak in Gascon? Winkelmeier had briefly shuffled through the book of ciphers the State Department had given him on his last visit home, but that gave no clues at all, not even about operations code-named 'Kagemusha'. Yes, he would simply have to wait and see and play it all by ear, make it up as he went along, just like the band on the runway appeared to be doing with his cherished national anthem.

The aircraft appeared as a black speck on the horizon at the exact same moment as Hakim Akim's calvacade sped through the airport gates and drove out on to the tarmac. The President descended from the second car in line, right in front of Winkelmeier and, getting out, shook the Ambassador's hand. He asked in Bangistani, translated by the young interpreter from the Palace, "Who the hell are you?"

Winkelmeier laughed.

"Please tell His Excellency I am grateful that he could come and greet President Rump in person. This gesture will be greatly appreciated and will ensure a wonderful start to the summit."

President Akim had already turned away before the interpreter finished conveying Winkelmeier's words. He had seen a group of thirty or forty soldiers, carrying swords and flags, traipsing towards them from a barrack house next to the terminal, and began shouting violently at them. Unasked, the interpreter shared his commands with the Ambassador.

"Great Leader tell them, This isn't a fucking picnic, you dirty scum! Get your asses over here on the double or you'll be firing-squad practice targets before the day's finished."

"Very encouraging, good for morale," Winkelmeier told him, smiling, as he watched the guard of honor break into a sprint, all the while bowing, clutching their brass chamber-pot helmuts with one hand and their swords and flags, as best they could, with the other. Only as the airplane touched down on the runway was a semblance of order established, with the guards lined up facing their band colleagues.

Blakely and Schurz had spent much of the six-hour flight briefing Marie-Pierre on what to expect in Petrobangorski, while simultaneously endeavoring, without much success, to get her to ease up on the champagne. She had nothing at all to learn from them about drinking, however, after a life on the farm with Gaston, and they soon gave up this ambition and let her slug it back at her own ryhthm. For the rest, they assured her that the deal was already in the bag and that the visit was largely ceremonial. She should not be surprised, they told her, if she was treated with deference and high regard. The Bangistani didn't get many foreign guests and their visit was a rare event of some importance.

The jet doors opened and an arm reached out, pointed at Winkelmeier and summoned him to come up the aircraft stairs. The band struck up its dissonant and chaotic din but was quickly silenced by its leader who bawled at them that he was giving the orders and they should start when he said so.

Inside the plane, whose doors had been closed again, O'Reilly, Ormrod, Blakely and Schurz all huddled around Winkelmeier, who was briefly introduced to Marie-Pierre as the company's East Asia representative. O'Reilly took charge.

"Ambassador, it's a lot to grasp in three minutes, but this is the picture. We are here with two objectives. The first, as you know, is to conclude and sign a peace agreement in which Akim destroys all his nuclear weapons and missile development programmes, in exchange for a very major aid contribution from the US and its closest allies for the next several years. That's one reason why the British Foreign Minister is here with us on the trip. You have led us to believe that Akim's demands about the withdrawal of our nukes from Europe could be taken off the table if the price is right. Is that so?"

"Everything that he's told me leads me to that assessment, yes, Sir. This is a man obsessed above and beyond all else with the accumulation of vast wealth beyond any normal man's wildest dreams. You remember Mansu Musa?"

"We do indeed, Winkelmeier. The King of Mali. So, fingers crossed, we can get a deal on that front. The second objective is to get our doppelgänger in and out of Petrobangorski without her doubting for a second that the mass production of zucchini she is gearing up to cultivate will be bought by Bangistan. Blakely and Schurz here will be leading that parallel, simultaneous and completely fictitious negotiation. Is that clear? Any questions?"

"Why wouldn't it be clear?" laughed Winkelmeier nervously. "Just one question, really. Though Hakim Akim doesn't speak a word of English, as you know, he does of course have an interpreter, several in fact. One of them is here right now at the airport. How do we fool *him*."

"Good point. We shall tell him that President Rump speaks to us only in code, in order to keep his instructions and views confidential from our current adversaries and future great friends. The interpreter is in no position to cross-examine us on that, and Akim won't know the difference. Adela, please ask Madame Etxeberria a question, anything will do."

"L'òmi urós qu'ei lo qui se'n cred," Marie-Pierre responded.

"They'll be impressed," said Winkelmeier ironically. "What did you ask her, young lady?"

"I wanted to know if she felt well. She told me, 'The happy man is he who believes he is happy.' It's a Gascon proverb. A good one, I think, no?"

They all smiled.

"Let's go guys," said O'Reilly. "Adela, take Madame Etxeberria out first, please. That's the protocol, I think."

On a sign from its chief, the band struck up its cacophonous improvisation, breaking down three times after just a few notes, then setting off again from the beginning.

"What a bloody racket!" Marie-Pierre whispered to Adela.

"Ah, the Star-Mangled Stammer," quipped Schurz, provoking Blakely's giggles.

Hakim Akim stepped forward and shook Marie-Pierre's hand at the foot of the staircase. He stared deeply and coldly into her eyes, held her unmovable gaze for a few moments, and then burst into guffaws of laughter, slapping her back while he did so. She cast a questioning look at Adela, suggested that the President would "bust a gut, if he continues like that" and laughed too. They were off to a good start.

To immortalize the moment, the state television camera crew, which had been hanging about behind the band, was called forward to film a rerun of the scene. Akim grabbed Marie-Pierre's hand once more, shook it vigorously, and again thwacked her heartedly on the back. She was taller and stronger than him and, tired of being slapped around, gave him a great thump on the shoulder in return. He reeled back two or three steps. They laughed again.

The group split up among the limousines, Marie-Pierre accompanied in hers only by Adela and, for show, two of the CIA agents, and drove off to the Presidential Palace. The agreed programme was light for the first round of talks, particularly since it was now late afternoon. They would chat and get to know each other for an hour or so and then have dinner if they were up to it.

Much to the surprise of Blakely, Schurz and Co., Hakim Akim and his young interpreter were the only Bangistani representatives who showed up in the Palace meeting room. The President clearly wanted their discussions to remain private. Well, it certainly made things simpler, they thought.

Akim began with a handful of niceties about the pleasure he felt to finally meet the American President. It had been so much fun to insult each other on Twitter these past few months, he said. Now, they had serious matters to discuss. War must be avoided at all costs and there surely was a way to achieve that, he suggested with a heavy wink.

The version that arrived in Marie-Pierre's ears through the Bangistani-English-Gascon translation was slightly different.

"I loved your zucchini when my Consul brought me one from Paris. I have never tasted such zucchini in my life. I don't think that I can now live without them on my table. And I want my whole people to enjoy them too. So, we want to sign a very big contract for as many as you can grow and deliver to us."

Marie-Pierre got quickly to her main question.

"How much are you willing to pay per kilo and when do you need them? You can have a couple of tons this summer, with luck, and then we'll look at considerably increasing production next year, when we've cultivated our spare field."

After a little murmuring between Rump's advisors, Adela translated.

"The President thanks you for your warm welcome. He is a man who likes to get straight to the point. Yes, it was good to insult each other for a while. I enjoyed it as much as you. But now to business. We are not going to take our nuclear capabilities out of Europe. You can forget that right away. At the same time, I must say that we have no interest at all in deploying our weapons against your fine country. Our enemies are Russia and China, not Bangistan - as long as you give up your arsenal."

As Akim gave a cautious reply, saying notably that he couldn't afford Russia and China to be his enemies, Adela whispered a simultaneous translation to Marie-Pierre, renewing the President's awe of her zucchini and saying that he was prepared to pay a fair price if she could ensure regular supplies.

At this point, Madame Etxeberria turned to Blakely and urged him, "Show him the photographs! That'll get his appetite up for a deal."

With reluctance, Blakely reached into his briefcase and pulled out a sheaf of pictures.

He told Akim: "President Rump is anxious that you should see the latest generation of nuclear missiles that America now has placed in Europe to counter, most especially, Russia's growing imperialistic desires." And, with a lump in his throat, he handed the photographs to Akim.

The Bangistani President turned them every which way, scowled, looked twice through the set, scratched his chin and then glared sternly at Marie-Pierre.

"They look like zucchini!" said Akim, breaking into howls of laughter, clutching his sides, rocking back and forward in his chair. All this provoked the hilarity of his interpreter too and for a few minutes neither of them could speak.

"What's so funny?" enquired Marie-Pierre.

It was Ormrod who rushed to the rescue, whispering to Adela to tell her that Akim had made a rather naughty and primitive remark about the resemblance between her zucchini and a certain male appendage.

"That's not funny at all," retorted Marie-Pierre. "He can't be vulgar with me, you know."

Having made his good joke, Akim suggested that they should stop there and get down to serious discussions and negotiations in the morning. They agreed and declined his most cordial invitation to dine before they left for their hotel. They were tired after their long trip.

Marie-Pierre was a down-to-earth woman, and when she saw the Presidential suite on the top floor of the Petrobangorski Hilton, she was aghast.

"All of us have to sleep in *here*?" she asked Adela. "There are only two beds! One bathroom! And no privacy at all. Gaston wouldn't like it, you know."

Adela smiled and said that no, she had misunderstood, it was only for the two of them. The men were to sleep in their own rooms on the floor below.

In one of those rooms, that of O'Reilly, the men had gathered for a few drinks around a large plateau of goat's meat club sandwiches that all but Winkelmeier and the adventurous Schurz declined. They compared impressions of the day.

"Well, we're still in business," began Ormrod. "I'm astonished that we've got this far without any problems or doubts at all. And Akim seemed less of an ogre than I thought he would be, even though I'm aware that below all the laughter and bonhomie, he's a cruel monster of the first order."

"Yes, Operation Kagemusha has come a very long way already," said O'Reilly. "I frankly don't know what can stop us now. Akim seemed quite ready to do a deal with us, wasn't aggressive at all. I was pleasantly surprised. I had a bad moment with the zucchini photos, of course, but it seems he has a sense of humor of sorts too."

Winkelmeier listened patiently to all their assessments and analyses of the discussions so far. He spoke only when each had had his say and they turned, last, to him for an appraisal.

"The man we met wasn't Hakim Akim", said the Ambassador.

"What?" they asked in astonished chorus.

"No," said Winkelmeier. "They sent a double too; they had their own Kagemusha."

CHAPTER 24

A HUNTING LODGE IN THE FOREST

"I want to see the Geneva Convention," said Ronald Rump. "I'm sure it has something on political prisoners."

"Sorry, Sir, I don't happen to have a copy on me," said his American guard.

"Go and fucking get one, then, you goon. That's a command from your President. It may just avoid you the electric chair when you're convicted of treason!"

"I'm just following orders, Sir. Nothing and nobody is coming in or out of here."

Rump smiled.

"And whose orders might those be, soldier? The Democrats are in on this too, aren't they? That bunch of no-good foreign leaders couldn't have done this without traitors on our side too. Am I right?"

"Sorry, Sir, I'm not at liberty to discuss any of this."

"And you?" Rump asked the other guard, a Frenchman. "You and your President are boasting all the fucking time about being the home – 'la Patrie!' – of human rights. Is this how you respect them? Abducting the Head of State of another fucking nation?"

The French agent was less loquacious than his American colleague. He said nothing.

"Dumb-ass mute," muttered Rump.

The old hunting lodge lay deep in the Satory forest just to the south of the Palace. It was now used exclusively by the woodcutters and gardeners who took care of the Versailles Estate. They had all been given two weeks holiday, one before and one after the G7 summit. A temporary perimeter of barbed wire had been thrown up half a mile in all directions to keep out snooping ramblers.

The lodge was rudimentarily furnished, but adequate for its current purpose. Its salon had a table and a chair, a sofa and now two beds that had been dragged in from the adjoining bedroom. One of them was for President Rump; the other was for the guards, who took turns to sleep.

Though Rump's telephones had been removed from him, the President was not totally cut off from the outside world. His captors had decided that he could have a television, without which he might cause even more trouble than was absolutely necessary. It would also prepare him a little for the shock that was coming. A smart TV was thus installed with a VPN that made it possible to capture American channels. Agents had set it on Fox even before Rump had arrived. He was not allowed to touch the set himself, and couldn't anyhow, since he was permanently attached by handcuffs to either the heavy oak table or his bed.

"How long will you keep me here?" asked Rump, addressing the American agent again.

"It's not for me to say, Sir."

"Jesus. Does that thing work?" He pointed at the television in the corner.

"Indeed, Sir. I'll put it on if you like. Fox good enough? We have it directly from home, Sir."

"Well, there's the first good news of the day. Stick it on would you."

There was *breaking news*, as the jargon has it, at that very instant. The ticker stuttering across the bottom of the screen told the story.

The text read: "In a few moments, the President will arrive in Bangistan to seek peace."

"No he won't, suckers," laughed Rump. "He's sitting in a fucking hut in the middle of a French forest."

He spoke to his guards over his shoulder.

"See guys, a few minutes and the word will be out. I never got to Bangistan, so the question's gonna be – where the fuck am I? The world is going to be turned upside down to find me, you know. Big time."

The guards pointed at the television set behind him and he turned again to look at it. A group of people he didn't know were disembarking from a small aircraft. The studio anchor spoke.

"And here it is, the moment we've all been waiting for. President Ronald Rump steps on the runway of Akim Airport to be greeted by America's current chief foe, Hakim Akim. Peace, ladies and gentlemen, is hopefully at hand now. That is what we at Fox News pray for and we know that you will join us."

The images lasted no more than thirty seconds. Apart from himself, he recognized only one other man. He couldn't be sure, because of the bad quality of the pictures, but he was pretty certain it was O'Reilly of the CIA.

"I am *not* in Bangistan!," the President shouted.

"I'm sorry, Sir, but we'll have to put the tape back on your mouth unless you can keep it quiet," the American agent advised him.

"This is a bad dream, isn't it guys?" he said softly. "I haven't gone fucking crazy, have I? I am *not* in Bangistan, for Christ's sake. I am *here*. Aren't I?"

"As long as we are, you are," said the Frenchman soberly.

CHAPTER 25

THE PRICE IS FIXED

Hakim Akim called the Ambassador at daybreak, at "first bleat of goat", as Mrs Winkelmeier liked to joke. The Embassy was surrounded by livestock farms. The young interpreter was on the line too.

"You know it was not me yesterday, don't you Winkelmeier? I know you see many things."

"Yes, Your Excellency."

"What mistake did we make? How you know? He is very good double, don't you think? Perhaps my best."

"He didn't recognize me at the airport, Mr. President, he asked who I was."

"Idiot."

"But there was one other thing. I noticed he didn't scratch his index finger against the side of his thumb. You do it all the time, you know."

"I did not know that, Winkelmeier. But you right, I am doing it right now! You not fool, whatever people say."

The Ambassador chuckled timidly.

"Anyhow, I am sorry. It was not trick or something. I had terrible pain in back and I hate protocol. So I ask idiot to go for me, as usual in this situations. My translator told me mood was good."

"Indeed it was, Sir. We're all looking forward to this morning's session and, hopefully, a deal."

"Good. You don't tell Rump, others, it was not me?"

"Oh no, Sir. I didn't think we had anything at all to gain by that. I knew you would have your reasons and that it would just complicate matters if the others were aware of it."

"Good, Winkelmeier. Look, just one question before we all meet at ten. What your government spend every year?"

"Oh, about four and a half trillion dollars, I believe."

"What your GDP?"

"Something around twenty trillion, I think."

"And your debt?"

"A little more than that. I'd say around twenty-two trillion dollars, or close."

"Very good, Winkelmeier. That help me. See you later!"

And at that Akim hung up. Winkelmeier could quite clearly hear the distant, childhood cha-ching sounds of the cash register in his Uncle's grocery store in Brooklyn. He sighed.

They met in the same room as the previous day. Akim enquired politely if they had slept well and if they liked his hotel. They all murmured their thanks and approval.

Rather than at Hakim Akim, the men were all looking sideways at Winkelmeier for the agreed sign. He soon pulled up his right trouser leg to the calf and scratched. It was the President himself. They were on!

Akim reiterated his double's remarks of the previous day about past misunderstandings and, perhaps, intemperate language on both sides. How this had escalated into America's threats to take military action against Bangistan, even to unleash the terrible force of nuclear weapons, was beyond his understanding, but they had crossed the red line and he had been obliged to show them the might of his own power by the Caspian missile test.

In the meantime, Adela simultaneously whispered complete nonsense into Marie-Pierre's ears about the agricultural challenges of Bangistan and their dearth of many kinds of fruit and vegetables, most notably zucchini, which had once been grown in the country but had disappeared many years ago, wiped out by a particularly vicious plant virus.

Marie-Pierre responded, translated by Adela, prompted by O'Reilly, and then delivered falsely to Akim's interpreter. She expressed her regret about the disease – it was a constant battle everywhere, she said – but she was happy to be able to help them start afresh. What about the price? Could they discuss that?

This all came back to Hakim Akim as:

"We agree. Bygones are bygones. We don't want any more conflict and most certainly not war. Here's the deal we propose. Bangistan will destroy all its nuclear capabilities, as we've already set out, together with the means to rebuild them. All this to be verifiable, of course. The United States, in return, will no longer hold its missiles in readiness to strike Bangistan, as they are now, and promises that it will never take any measures of aggression against you as long as our agreement lasts. We suggest twenty years, to be reviewed after that time. President Rump asks, 'What about the price?' " At least that was true.

There was silence. Marie-Pierre thought that the time had come to take the initiative, to make her proposal. Nothing ventured, nothing gained. She held up three fingers.

"Three Euros a kilo. Not including transport or taxes or anything else. That's not my business."

Through the translation circuit went her proposal, changed on route by O'Reilly's instructions to Adela. Three hundred billion over the length of the twenty-year agreement.

Hakim Akim held up five fingers.

"What does that mean?" Marie-Pierre asked Adela.

"We're both Presidents, Akim," went the translation. "We have responsibilities to our people. They won't even begin to understand that we give such a huge amount of money to you, even over twenty years."

"Don't tell them then," said Akim. "It's none of their business."

"Things don't work like that in America, my friend."

"Tough. It's not twenty years, by the way. It's twenty days. We've already got a missile set up for the Black Sea if we don't get it by then."

In the parallel story, Hakim Akim was offering Marie-Pierre not three, but five Euros a kilo. She was cheating herself with her miserable price. She didn't realize what a treasure she had. The best zucchini ever tasted by man. And so on and so on.

"What a nice man," Marie-Pierre told Adela.

Ormrod suggested that they perhaps should adjourn the meeting for half an hour to allow President Rump and the whole delegation to discuss the financial demands in private.

"Good, I can take a piss," Akim told his interpreter. "Don't translate that," he added swiftly. He left the room and told them all they could stay there. He and the young man would be back in a short while.

O'Reilly suggested to Adela that she and Marie-Pierre should go for a short walk.

"Ambassador Winkelmeier, what do you think?" asked O'Reilly when they were alone. "You know this Akim far better than any of us. What are our chances of beating him down on the price? We can't possibly get our hands on money like that at short notice, nothing like it."

"If I know him, Sir, he won't budge an inch. I understand that the word 'compromise' doesn't even exist in the Bangistani language. He's simply not used to giving in to anybody. He's never had to do it in his life. I would guess that if you push on the five hundred billion, he'll make it six hundred."

"What do you think, Ormrod?" O'Reilly asked the Foreign Minister. "What leeway does the UK have in all this."

"It's a huge amount of money, of course. We can certainly come in on a part of it. And I'm sure that the others will too. It's really part of the pact that conjoins us. Everyone has an interest. Perhaps, at the end of the day, it'll actually be a small price to pay for the dozen other catastrophes that will be avoided if we can get Rump out of the way when all this is over. Peace and sanity are a lot less expensive for all of us than the madness of perpetual conflict."

"Hear, hear, George!" Blakely added.

"It's done, then," said O'Reilly. "Ambassador, have you printed out the draft deal I sent you? Can you add the figure by hand?"

Winkelmeier produced the Treaty of Peace Between the United States of America and the People's Popular Democratic Republic of Bangistan from his briefcase. He had copies both in English and in Bangistani. With trembling hand, he wrote in the sacred figure: Five Hundred Billion Dollars, inscribing it in English in the Bangistani version too.

Soon, Adela and Marie-Pierre returned.

"You're ready to sign for five Euros a kilo, then?" asked Blakely.

"It was more than I dreamt of, frankly," she replied. "It's going to mean a lot of work for me and Gaston – we plan already to take on a few seasonal workers – but with the tractor and the cold store we're confident that we can meet all requirements."

When Adela had translated, all the men smiled and clapped.

"Tell him that you accept," Adela nudged Marie-Pierre when Akim and the interpreter returned. She obliged.

"Wonderful, wonderful, my friends, I knew that you would see reason. Mr. President, I shall discuss details with your excellent man Winkelmeier, most notably information on my, I mean 'our', bank accounts in various places."

"And, of course, the plans for the immediate destruction of your all nuclear capabilities," added O'Reilly, without going through Marie-Pierre.

"Of course, of course," said Akim. "I am so happy. Let's go and toast our new friendship! America and Bangistan! Allies forever! Shit on China! Shit on Russia! Your enemies are our enemies!"

Marie-Pierre and Akim signed each of the two documents, immortalized by the camera crew called in by the interpreter. Each took a copy away. Marie-Pierre gave hers to Blakely for safekeeping. At some point, unknown to her, it would magically be transformed into the Etxeberria-Akim Zucchini Production and Export Agreement.

The camera crew were unceremoniously dismissed from the room as a dozen white-clad, bowtied waiters glided in, pushing carts overflowing with great bowls of caviar, steaming blinis, and vast cream cakes.

"Caviar at last!" cried Schurz. "I've never seen so much of it in my life. Is it really sturgeon, Ambassador?"

"Yes, young man. They don't give a hoot for the fishing ban, of course. Akim gets his directly from the rivers in the north of the country. I have to confess that it is exquisite."

The champagne flowed too. Only the best that Reims could produce.

Hakim Akim was again suffering from back pain and apologized to the group.

"I would love to say goodbye at airport, but alas I have other engagements. I know that your Ambassador will take care of final arrangements with my staff. I wish you a good trip home to America, my new favorite country!"

And that was that. He departed, only stopping to whisper a few words in the Ambassador's ears.

"I love you, Winkelmeier."

Three hours later, they were in the air, bound for Paris.

CHAPTER 26

PEACE IN OUR TIME, PART 2

O'Reilly, flanked by Haubois and Pensec, who suggested that they deserved to be in on the priceless moment, crept through the woodland, accompanied by the three CIA agents who had made the trip to Petrobangorski.

The return flight from Bangistan had landed discretely at the nearby Saint-Cyr military school aerodrome. Two cars took them to the forest edge.

Agents were waiting to open a breach in the barbed wire. A few hundred yards on, they entered the hunting lodge. Rump had been extremely, noisily obstreperous that day, and his guards had been obliged to tape his mouth once more.

O'Reilly gave a sign of the hand for the removal of the gag, pulled up a chair and sat facing Rump.

The President, whose arms were tied behind his own chair, unexpectedly smiled.

"So, I was right. That was really *you* I saw on Bangistani TV," said Rump. "I always knew you were the traitor, O'Reilly. How much did the Democrats pay you, huh?"

O'Reilly said nothing; he let the President speak.

"You're dead, you know, Mister CIA Director. Just for you, we're gonna track down the most incompetent, cruel executioner, in a county in the heart of Trumpland, and give him the job of consigning you to hell. What do you think about *that*?"

"I have my doubts that's going to happen, Mr President. I'll tell you our alternative plan."

He handed him two sheets of paper.

"We're going right now to Orly Airport, where four hundred journalists and countless camera crews are awaiting your return from Bangistan. A news conference is going to start exactly two hours from now and you are going to read this statement. We *might* let you answer a couple of questions, because we think that you are sufficiently full of bullshit to answer them convincingly. Sir."

Rump read the paper. Peace in our time. Great deal. Bangistan to abandon all weapons. Historic victory for America. Only I could achieve this, etc. etc.

"It's nice, no?" asked O'Reilly.

"You must be out of your fucking mind," said Rump. "As soon as I'm out of this forest, I'm going to denounce you and all your accomplices, have you arrested, put in chains, and then shipped back to America for trial. Then I'll start thinking about what I am going to do with our allies and those sons-of-bitches who abducted me on your behalf."

"Let me lay it out for you real simple, Rump, you bone-headed moron," said O'Reilly, for once dropping his habitual, deferential vocabulary. "You have two options: One. You stand up in front of the world's press, denounce a plot against you and against America, say you never went to Petrobangorski, never signed any deal, have in fact spent the last forty-eight hours in a hut in the French woods, blame the CIA, and say you're ripping up the peace agreement with Akim."

"Damn right. That's exactly what I'm going to say!"

"At which point, of course, the media, not being quite as dumb as you think, will ask: OK. But who *was* that we saw on television, arriving at Akim Airport, signing the peace deal? Who *did* negotiate an end to the conflict between the United States and Bangistan? Who *did* win peace? At this moment, perhaps, your loyal servant O'Reilly, who accompanied you, will inform the journalists: 'Actually, it wasn't the President at all, he's right. It was a peasant woman who sells zucchini in her village near the Pyrenees.'"

Rump was silent for a few minutes. He finally said, "Doesn't look good, does it? For me, for America, for any of us ... Do you have an alternative?"

"Yes, *Sir*! Glad you asked. This is the other narrative. After two days of really tough negotiations, employing all your remarkable skills as a *deal-maker*, you wrested from the jaws of defeat and conflict a most wondrous, unexpected, *historic* and practically impossible result that none of your predecessors – even though they had never heard of Bangistan, but don't mention that, of course – could possibly have achieved. 'Peace in our time.' You can actually say it. Zebreski was wrong about that. No one alive today in America has even heard of Chamberlain and will make no parallels at all. I'd skip the 'Ich Bin Ein Bangistani', though. Nobody in America speaks German and they've forgotten that too. We have no sense of history at all, when I think about it."

"Is that it?" asked Rump.

"Not quite, Sir."

"And?"

"You are finished, of course. You can see out your term, but that's it. We've all had enough, frankly. What we *shall* do is to try and get you the Nobel Peace Prize; we are certain, at least, that you will be welcomed back in the States as a real hero. We're organising that. So, it's an easy choice, isn't it Rump? You were kidnapped and, while held in the woods, peace was negotiated in your place by a French peasant woman - not that anyone will believe you. Or, you did it personally for America and the world, at great risk to your person, and will go down in history as a conqueror."

"You've got me by the balls, haven't you?"

"I think that's a good way of putting it, *Sir*."

*

Blakely, Schurz and Ormrod stood at the back of the vast hall at Orly Airport commandeered for Rump's news conference for the world's media.

O'Reilly spotted them as he entered the hall at Rump's side, accompanied by two dozen Secret Service agents who had recuperated their President, in some confusion, a little earlier. The CIA Director winked and smiled.

The President read to script. Word for word. He had achieved peace. He had saved the world from conflict. Only he could have done it. No one had believed it possible.

And a lot of other self-promoting baloney cooked up by a joyous band of jokers on a Gulfstream jet from Petrobangorski.

CHAPTER 27

A PARADE IN NEW YORK

They ate zucchini, brought by Adela as a gift from Marie-Pierre.

Blakely was in the kitchen, as usual. Ruth greeted the guests, O'Reilly, Ormrod, Schurz, Adela, and gave them drinks.

"Roast goat. Everyone fine with that?" asked Blakely, emerging from the kitchen.

They all laughed.

"No. Duck, actually. That's where it all started, wasn't it Scott? Do you remember?"

"The duck, yes, I remember well. I don't recall the conversation that evening, though."

"Unlikely," said Ruth.

Soon, as they ate their *magret de canard aux courgettes*, Ruth got up and turned on the television, as planned.

"CNN OK?" she asked.

"No, no," everyone protested. "We want Fox, we want Fox," they chanted in unison.

"Let's drink the poison from the chalice until the very last drop," said O'Reilly.

Rump's calvacade drove slowly along lower Broadway, the man himself erect and waving from his open-top limousine as an immense storm of ticker tape showered down upon him and the line of cars.

"What are the crowd shouting?" asked Ruth.

"Four More Beers! Four More Beers! I think," said Schurz.

"I take the hint. I'll get them," laughed Blakely.

"The Canyon of Heroes, as they call that stretch of road, is today the Graveyard of Zeroes," said O'Reilly philosophically. "It's the end. And we did it. Christ, I'm a happy man today," he said with great emotion.

The conquering hero had returned to America. He would never again leave its shores.

CHAPTER 28

WHAT HAPPENED THEN

A lot happened in the next few months.

Almost immediately, there was a secret emergency meeting of the *Chefs de Cabinet* of the leaders of the G7 nations, without America. They had one agenda item only. How much money could they raise for the Bangistan peace accord to support their US friends? When they had completed their deliberations, and consulted their leaders, they cabled the results of their efforts to Washington, where the information was shared by only two men, President Rump and CIA Director O'Reilly.

Simultaneously, Winkelmeier was summoned to the Presidential Palace in Petrobangorski once more and handed a long list of the Akim family accounts in two dozen offshore and onshore tax havens.

The funds were all transfered within ten days, the great bulk coming from the United States itself, facilitated by a little-known executive capacity to order the payment of unbudgeted funds in the case of national emergencies, regardless of the effects on the national deficit.

Assured that the money was in the bank, or rather *banks*, Hakim Akim ordered the identification and collection of every ounce of trinitrotoluene, dynamite and all other combustible substances in the nation. Within a week, it had been gathered and then transported by more than five hundred trucks to the Kalimari Mountains. A thousand soldiers and explosives experts labored for two weeks to set it in place for detonation.

Yogi Akim himself pushed the button from his post two miles away, with Winkelmeier at his side. It was quite a spectacle. Not only was the immense cave system reduced to a great mass of rubble, but the Kalimari foothills themselves changed shape; they were practically flattened. For good measure, and an even better show for the US Ambassador, Akim, as Minister of Defence, then sent in all the available warplanes in the Bangistani Air Force to unload every conventional bomb they could put their hands on.

"It's over, Winkelmeier," said Yogi Akim. "We cannot threaten you any longer. There goes all our capacity to be nuisance to the United States."

Peace had finally been achieved.

Sir Stephen Blakely became the second youngest knight of the Queen's realm in the modern era, just three months senior to a Scottish tennis player. He was confidentially assured that the Paris Embassy was his in due course, above all when the Foreign Office could rid themselves of a certain philandering ambassador who was hanging on for his life to the post.

George Ormrod, as expected, became Prime Minister and today, still, is hugely popular, an unusual fate for any politician in our times. He still cannot spell Kyrgyzstan, but that's a lot less important in his new job.

Scott and Adela Schurz are married. He left the foreign service and they are now raising sheep on their farm in the Aldudes valley on the banks of the River Nive, just south of Saint-Jean-Pied-de-Port. Adela is expecting a child, whose first language will, it goes without saying, be Gascon.

Marie-Pierre Etxeberria, for the first time in many years, slipped from gold to bronze in the zucchini category of the regional agricultural prizes. The highly prejudiced judges, jealous of her export business, shook their heads in feigned sorrow, and lamented the deficiences of mass productivity over quality.

Monsieur Lizarazu has been elected to a seventh term as mayor of Luzère-Les-Bains.

O'Reilly is still head of the CIA. There have to be advantages, after all, in being in possession of all the secrets worth knowing in the world.

Holden has quit the Department of State. He is now CEO of a conservative think tank seeking to promote fascist regimes in Europe and South America.

*

Yogi Akim came to see the Winkelmeiers off at the airport. They were returning to Washington for good.

"We fooled you, you know, Ambassador?"

"Oh, in what way?"

"We had no missiles or warheads at all. We sold them all, not a single one left. All those fireworks in the Kalimari Mountains? We were blowing up empty caves."

Winkelmeier smiled. He didn't know and didn't care whether Akim was telling the truth or not. But he did add:

"We fooled you too, Akim. It wasn't Rump who came to Petrobangorski. It wasn't Rump who met Hakim. Your brother signed a peace deal with a French peasant - a woman, in addition. She cultivates zucchini."

*

A few months later, Yogi Akim died in a most unfortunate accident on a building construction site in Petrobangorski. He was sauntering around the top floor of the forthcoming Akim Tower Hotel when a section gave way underneath him and he plunged thirty-five storeys to the ground. A police enquiry is still in process and is not predicted to ever be concluded.

Ambassador Winkelmeier has retired and has joined the Board of Human Rights Watch. He has never felt more fulfilled in his life. He advises, most particularly, on the re-emergence of concentration camps in the world. His parents died in Auschwitz. He can remember nothing about them. This is his way of sustaining their memory.

Throughout that summer, a giant truck pulled up in front of the Etxeberria's farm once a week, loaded up a ton or two of zucchini, and drove off again. It was driven by an agent of the French intelligence services, a certain Pierre Morand – but not very far. About fifty miles north of Luchère-Les-Bains, a huge pit had been dug in an isolated part of the lower Pyrenees forest. It was here that the zucchini found their last resting place. After two harvests, two summers, Morand would come no more. It had been quite the weirdest assignment he had ever been asked to undertake.

Hakim Akim still reigns in Bangistan. He hasn't yet made his *hajj*, his pilgrimage to Mecca, but still has every intention of doing so. Having finally overseen the building of a Bangistan telecommunications network worthy of its name, he now spends his days on the telephone speaking to hedge fund managers and the Heads of State of fiscal paradises.

Before he retires, O'Reilly has set himself a single objective – to get America's money back. His agents and investigators are already snooping around a number of notorious tax havens. He personally leads the Ireland team, in honor of his ancestors.

Shortly before the election, President Rump announced, to general astonishment, that he would abandon his bid for a second term.

A few weeks later, he was admitted to the Palm Beach Rest Home, an asylum for the demented rich, where he is reliably reported to be regaling the inmates with stories of his decisive meeting and "great deal" with Hakim Akim. "It got

me the Nobel Prize, you know", is apparently his most repeated phrase.

This was a lie.

Neither Ronald Rump nor Hakim Akim received the
Nobel Prize for Peace as they, indeed the whole world, had
fully expected. An indiscrete member of the Norwegian
Nobel Committee later confided to a few journalists that
while these nominations had been given due consideration,
the members felt that the Prize had been awarded to "a sufficient number of swines and butchers already."

Instead, the laureate that year was, surprisingly enough,
a nineteen-year-old gorilla called Malabo. According to the
Committee's Secretary, announcing the Prize in a news conference, the ape was selected as an exceptional symbolic gesture, to "highlight and honor the dignified, pacific and noble
nature of our friends in the animal kingdom in contrast to
our own most terrible, violent and malevolent species."

Malabo, brought from his cage in Madrid Zoo for the
award, disgraced himself scandalously while receiving his
cheque and scroll from King Harald at the award ceremony
in Oslo City Hall.

But that, ladies and gentlemen, my dear readers, is another story …

ABOUT THE AUTHOR

Born in 1954 in London of mixed Scottish and English parentage, Timothy Balding grew up and was educated on a British military base in Germany. He left school and his family at the age of sixteen to return alone to the United Kingdom, where he was hired as a reporter on local newspapers in Reading in the county of Berkshire. For the ensuing decade, he worked on local and regional titles and then at Press Association, the national news agency, covering politics in Westminster, the British Parliament. He exiled himself to Paris, France, in 1980, and spent the next thirty years working for international, non-governmental organizations. For twenty-five of these, he was Chief Executive Officer of the World Association of Newspapers, the representative global group of media publishers and editors, established after World War II to defend the freedom and independence of the press worldwide. A Knight (First Class) in the Order of the White Rose of Finland—an honor accorded him by Nobel Peace laureate Martti Ahtisaari, former Finnish President— Timothy Balding currently lives in the Basque region of France and devotes himself to writing.

ALSO AVAILABLE FROM UWSP

- *November Rose: A Speech on Death* by Kathrin Stengel
  (2008 Independent Publisher Book Award)
- *November-Rose: Eine Rede über den Tod* by Kathrin Stengel
- *Philosophical Fragments of a Contemporary Life* by Julien David
- *17 Vorurteile, die wir Deutschen gegen Amerika und die Amerikaner
  haben und die so nicht ganz stimmen können* by Misha Waiman
- *The DNA of Prejudice: On the One and the Many* by Michael Eskin
  (2010 Next Generation Indie Book Award for Social Change)
- *Descartes' Devil: Three Meditations* by Durs Grünbein
- *Fatal Numbers: Why Count on Chance* by Hans Magnus
  Enzensberger
- *The Vocation of Poetry* by Durs Grünbein (2011 Independent
  Publisher Book Award)
- *Mortal Diamond: Poems* by Durs Grünbein
- *Yoga for the Mind: A New Ethic for Thinking and Being & Meridians
  of Thought* by Michael Eskin & Kathrin Stengel (2014 Living
  Now Book Award)
- *Health Is In Your Hands: Jin Shin Jyutsu – Practicing the Art of Self-
  Healing (With 51 Flash Cards for the Hands-on Practice of Jin Shin
  Jyutsu)* by Waltraud Riegger-Krause (2015 Living Now Book
  Award for Healing Arts)
- *The Wisdom of Parenthood: An Essay* by Michael Eskin
- *A Moment More Sublime: A Novel* by Stephen Grant (2015
  Independent Publisher Book Award for Contemporary Fiction)
- *High on Low: Harnessing the Power of Unhappiness* by Wilhelm
  Schmid (2015 Living Now Book Award for Personal Growth &
  2015 Independent Publisher Book Award for Self-Help)
- *Become a Message: Poems* by Lajos Walder (2016 Benjamin Franklin
  Book Award for Poetry)
- *What We Gain As We Grow Older: On Gelassenheit* by Wilhelm
  Schmid (2016 Living Now Gold Award)
- *On Dialogic Speech* by L. P. Yakubinsky

- *Passing Time: An Essay on Waiting* by Andrea Köhler
- *In Praise of Weakness* by Alexandre Jollien
- *Vase of Pompeii: A Play* by Lajos Walder
- *Below Zero: A Play* by Lajos Walder
- *Tyrtaeus: A Tragedy* by Lajos Walder
- *The Complete Plays* by Lajos Walder
- *Homo Conscius: A Novel* by Timothy Balding
- *Spanish Light: A Novel* by Stephen Grant
- *On Language & Poetry* by L. P. Yakubinsky
- *Philosophical Truffles* by Michael Eskin
- *The Complete Poems* by Lajos Walder (Bilingual Edition)
- *Összes Versei* by Vándor Lajos
- *The Man Who Couldn't Stop Thinking: A Novel* by Timothy Balding
- *Of Parents and Children: Tools for Nurturing a Lifelong Relationship* by Jorge & Demián Bucay
- *The Impostors: A Novel* by Timothy Balding
- *The Zucchini Conspiracy: A Novel of Alternative Facts* by Timothy Balding